SAVING NOAH

Lucinda Berry

Published in the United States by Rise Press

ISBN-10: 1976189934
ISBN-13: 978-1976189937

DEDICATION

To my love

1

Noah being charged as a sex offender sucker punched our entire suburban community. Child molesters were adults—dirty old men who lured children into their cars with promises of candy and treats. They weren't A-honor roll students who ran varsity track and went to mass every Sunday. I still cringed inside every time I said it, but our nightmare was finally about to be over.

Noah was getting out of the Marsh Foundation in three weeks and I'd counted every day that he'd been gone until he could come home again. I pulled two of his boxes out of the garage before my husband, Lucas, got home, hoping their presence would force him to talk about Noah's homecoming. I put them in a neat stack next to the couch, but when he walked into the living room, he skirted around them as if they weren't there, just like he dodged anything related to Noah.

After he tucked our youngest, Katie, into bed, he planted himself in front of the TV with the remote control in one hand and his phone in the other, shifting his attention back and forth between the two screens. I stared at him from the kitchen, trying to muster up the strength to approach him. He wasn't classically handsome but he'd always been attractive to me. The dimples in both cheeks made him look playful despite his khaki pants and buttoned-up shirt. He was six feet tall with a leanness that passed as athletic years ago, but decades working in an office had taken a toll on his body. His muscles had begun to sag and the bulge hanging over his belt grew more and more pronounced each year. I took a deep breath before heading into the living room to join him.

I plopped down on the couch next to him and did my best to appear relaxed. I crossed and uncrossed my legs, rearranged the magazines on the coffee table, and wiped away imaginary crumbs as I worked up the nerve to bring up the subject he continually avoided. I took another deep breath.

"Do you think we could talk?" I asked.

He stared at the screen in his hand without looking up. "Sure."

"About Noah."

His body stiffened the same way it did each time I mentioned his name.

"What's there to talk about?" he asked.

There was no way he didn't know Noah was getting out soon no matter how hard he tried to remain oblivious to what was happening with his case.

"Come on, Lucas. Don't be difficult."

"I'm not being difficult. What's there to talk about?"

"Maybe the fact that your son is getting out of treatment in three weeks, and we haven't discussed what we're going to do about it?"

"You already know how I feel about it."

"But that was a year ago. We haven't talked about it since."

I had ignored him when he'd said he didn't want Noah to come home after treatment. It was only two months since he'd been locked up and his discharge date was so far into the future that it was the least of my concerns. I was worried about how he'd survive being locked up with criminals and sexual deviants, how he'd sleep in a strange place, and if they would feed him food he liked. Wondering what we'd do when he got out was the last thing on my mind.

"I still feel the same way," he said, his eyes glued to his phone. I wanted to slap it out of his hand.

"Are you serious?" I tried to keep my voice calm.

He let out a deep sigh. "I don't want to get into it with you again. Please, don't start this."

"Start this? I'm not trying to *start* anything. We have to prepare and figure out what we're going to do. This is happening, whether you want it to or not. I've given you time to pretend like he doesn't exist, but you're not going to be able to anymore. Not when he's here. You're going to have to see him and, God forbid, you might even have to talk to him."

When Noah first got locked up, I forced Lucas to come with me on the weekend visits and family sessions because the treatment staff stressed the critical role families played in the rehabilitation process. Lucas was an affectionate man, but he could barely bring himself to touch Noah during our visits. He shook his hand with the formality of meeting a business acquaintance for the first time. He rarely looked at him; his eyes slid over him before he looked away, unable to hide his contempt and disgust. He only spoke when spoken to during the family sessions and sat mute whenever we met with Noah alone.

I breathed a sigh of relief the first time he pretended to be sick so he wouldn't have to go. Even though all the experts told us how important family support was for Noah's recovery, I didn't think a father who looked at him like he was a pariah qualified. It was better that I went alone. The next weekend rolled around, and he said he needed to stay home with Katie to work on her science project, and I happily agreed. He didn't bother to make up an excuse the next week, and I pretended not to notice. We didn't speak about it again. I went alone each Sunday, and he never asked about the visit when I got back. It wasn't long before his silence extended to all things concerning Noah.

I tried not to be angry about Lucas's attitude toward him. His response was better than some fathers'. He didn't react like Jamar Pickney's father, who'd shot his son in the head when he learned he'd been sexually abusing his sister, or the father in Detroit who'd slit his son's throat for taking naked pictures of his cousins and selling them online.

There were only two fathers who attended the groups at Marsh. Most of the kids didn't have fathers in their lives before their offenses, and the ones that were there either emotionally detached after their sons' convictions or disappeared. The moms I met assured me men processed their emotions about it differently. They were confident Lucas just needed space to deal with things in his own way and would come around eventually, so I'd given him his space but his period of avoidance was over.

"Okay. Let's talk about where he's going to live," he said. He turned off the TV and laid his phone on the coffee table.

"He's seventeen, where else is he supposed to live?" I couldn't keep the emotion out of my voice no matter how hard I tried.

“We could help him become an emancipated minor. I already looked into the process. It’s pretty easy, especially if the parents are on board with it. All you have to do is fill out an application saying that all parties agree to the emancipation and go before a judge to put his stamp of approval on it. Then, he’s free to live on his own. It’s that simple.” Unlike me, his voice was devoid of all emotion.

“Really? How’s he supposed to live on his own? What kind of a job is he going to get when he doesn’t have a high school diploma? And did you forget he’ll be a registered sex offender? He’s not even going to be able to use the Internet.”

“He’ll have to figure it out.”

How was he going to do that without any help? How could Lucas consider sending him into the world alone when he didn’t have any of the basic skills he needed to survive? He was still a kid.

He took my hand in his. “I know you love him and how hard this must be for you.”

I jerked my hand away. “I love him? What about you? You act like he’s some stranger. Like he’s not even your son. He’s still your son, Lucas.”

“He stopped being my son when he raped those girls.” His lips were set in a straight line.

“He didn’t rape them, don’t say that,” I snapped.

There was a difference between rape and what he did. He touched the girls, but he didn’t rape them. Rape was different, and I clung to anything separating Noah from being a monster. He made a mistake. That was all. One mistake. We all made mistakes in adolescence.

"Calm down," he said.

I didn't want to calm down. I wanted him to care about his son the way I did—the way he used to. It was like nothing before mattered, and he'd erased all the memories he used to cherish. How could he forget the way he cried when Noah was born, or sat up with him all night in the shower when he had croup? He squealed like a child when Noah took his first steps and taught him to ride his bike without training wheels when he was only four years old. How could he dismiss the way his heart swelled with joy the first time he called him Daddy and every other milestone along the way? He'd coached his baseball team every summer since T-ball and never missed a swimming competition, even during tax season, when he was the busiest. He used to have an entire wall in his office devoted to Noah's artwork. It traced the lineage of his childhood, from the finger paintings he did in preschool to the self-portrait he created in junior high art class. Now, those images were gone, torn down, and all that remained was a blank wall with leftover pieces of tape hinting at the story the wall used to tell.

Lucas couldn't see past what he'd done, but I could. He was our son, and we couldn't wash our hands of him. Society was going to throw him away, but we couldn't.

"How can you make him live somewhere else? It's so cruel."

"I'm protecting my family." His jaw was set. The same angular line as Noah.

"He's your family and if you'd gone to any of the family meetings you'd know how important it is for us to be there for him. All the statistics say family support is one of the biggest factors in his recovery. It's the most important thing. We have to help him, offer him encouragement. It's what—"

"I can't have him under our roof. I won't put Katie in danger."

Anxiety curled in my stomach at the mention of her—our Peanut. She'd never gotten out of the twenty-fifth percentile on the growth charts. She was dainty and delicate with a small face and piercing blue eyes, constantly studying and taking in the world around her. Unlike most babies of the family, she hid from the limelight, painfully shy, and never liked to be the center of attention.

I rolled my eyes, shaking my head. "He'd never hurt Katie. Never."

"She's the same age as those girls."

"Yes, but he's better now." I said it with conviction, hoping my words had the power to make it true. "I'm meeting with the treatment team on Tuesday to come up with a safety plan. You should come with me."

He raised his eyebrows. "If he's better now, then why do we need a safety plan?"

He didn't understand. Part of a safety plan was keeping him out of situations where he might look guilty even if he was innocent.

"We can put locks on her doors just like we did before. We could even put a lock on his door too. Maybe one that locks from the outside, and we can make sure they're never alone together."

He scooted down the couch and put his arm around my shoulders. "Listen to yourself. Do you hear what you're saying? Locks on doors? Constant supervision? And putting a lock on the outside of his door? So, we'd basically lock him in his room every night and let him out in the morning like a prisoner? What kind of a life is that for him? For any of us?"

I bit my cheek to keep from crying. I hated this. Every part of it. It never got easier.

We sat in silence, staring at the blank TV screen, lost in thought about what our life used to be and the family we'd been, all the dreams we had for our kids and each other. The vortex of depression threatened to pull me inside, but I wasn't going back. I'd spiraled there before and crawled my way out. I wasn't doing it again.

"I can't let him live on his own. He's still just a kid." The tears I'd been holding back spilled down my cheeks.

"You could live with him."

I jerked my head up. "What are you talking about?"

"The two of you could get a place together. It could be somewhere nearby so you'd still be able to see Katie whenever you wanted to." He took a deep breath.

"Are you kidding me?" I jumped up, threw his arm off me, and paced the living room. We couldn't separate our family. We'd been apart long enough. I'd waited eighteen months for this day to come. He knew how excited I was for Noah to come home and all of us to be together again. How could he be so insensitive?

"I know it sounds crazy, but it's not if you stop to think about it. The other night I watched a documentary about a family who had a daughter with schizophrenia. She was psychotic and violent. She had a younger brother and started attacking him whenever she went into one of her fits. They couldn't live together anymore because they were afraid she'd hurt him, so they moved into two different apartments in the same complex. One where the girl stayed and another where the boy stayed. The parents went back and forth between them. They still spent time together as a family, but it kept the boy safe."

I couldn't believe we were talking about keeping Katie safe from Noah. He adored her from the moment we told him he was going to be a big brother. He was ten when she was born and insisted on learning how to do everything to care for her. He changed her diapers like a pro and fed her bottles like he'd been doing it his whole life. We were so grateful for the extra set of hands during those early months because unlike Noah, Katie was a difficult baby who didn't like to go to sleep without a fight and never slept for more than a few hours.

He spent hours lying next to her, reading her books, and dangling toys over her head. She was mesmerized by him, and he quickly became her favorite person. Her eyes searched for him whenever she heard his voice and toddled after him from room to room after she learned to walk. Her first word was "No-nah" and sometimes she still referred to him by it.

Unlike Lucas, Katie begged to go with me every week to see him, but staff only allowed siblings to visit on prearranged monthly outings. She created a calendar with her visiting days circled in pink hearts and tacked it on the bulletin board in her room. Each week she created care packages for me to take filled with letters she'd written and pictures she'd drawn for him. When she was able to visit, she gave him a huge hug and cried all the way home when we left. She was going to be as devastated as me if he didn't come home to live with us. How would we explain it?

She didn't know what he'd done. Not in words. At least we told ourselves that. She knew he made bad decisions and hurt kids because his brain wasn't working right at the time. We told her he had to go away so he could work with doctors to fix his brain and help him make better choices in the future. What would we tell her now?

How would I function away from her? Noah's absence sucked the energy out of me, but she breathed new life into me. She was the reason I got out of bed in the morning when all I wanted to do was pull the covers over my head and stay there. Her schedule organized my life and kept me grounded when everything spiraled out of control. I was determined to keep her sheltered from the tragedy as best I could and protect her innocence as long as possible, so I put on a brave face and worked hard to keep up with her routines and maintain the order in her life.

What would I do without fixing peanut butter and jelly sandwiches for her lunch or making sure her leotard was clean for ballet? How would I go to sleep without the angel kisses I placed on her forehead each night? What would she do when her nightmares startled her awake, and I wasn't there to lay with her and rub her back until she fell back to sleep?

Noah would suffer from her absence too. She was the only person who could make him smile and bring life to his eyes no matter how badly he felt. It wouldn't be lost on him that we didn't trust him enough to live in the house with his sister. What kind of a message did that send for his recovery?

But in the last eighteen months, I'd learned I was much stronger than I thought. I'd been blessed with an easy life and never would've thought I was capable of going through what I'd been through and not being devastated beyond repair. There weren't any parenting books about what to do when your son was a sex offender, and I'd figured it out on my own. It was like stumbling through a dark hallway alone, feeling your way through, and hoping for a glimmer of light to reveal your next step. It was too much to hope for a light at the end of the tunnel. I gave up on that long ago, but if I looked hard enough, there was always light on my next step. Was Lucas right? Was this the next step for our family?

I let out the breath I didn't realize I was holding.

"Okay," I said. "How would it work?"

2

I surveyed the two-bedroom apartment that would soon be my new home with Noah. I hadn't lived in an apartment since college and had forgotten how small they were. I took the unit even though it was on one of the busiest streets because it was within walking distance to Lucas's house. I already thought of it as his house. The carpet was beat up and worn, stained with patches of other people's lives. The walls had been a dingy grey covered in a yellowish film from the previous owners' smoking, but I'd talked the landlord into allowing me to paint the place. It was an easy sell because I promised to buy the paint and do it myself. The fresh coat of white on the walls looked nice and helped with the smell.

I painted Noah's room white too. I had considered painting it a different color, but didn't want to assume his favorite color was still blue. I would let him choose whatever color he liked, and we could paint it together as a weekend project after he was settled. I'd done my best to make his room look inviting despite how tiny it was.

When we were forced out of our home in Buffalo Grove after

his conviction, Lucas put all of his stuff in boxes and never moved them into the new house. They stayed stacked in the garage, the only boxes unmarked. It was like stepping back in time as I sorted through his things. I pulled out trophies and ribbons from his track meets and swimming matches. He was a natural athlete and excelled at sports. We used to joke that he was adopted since Lucas and I were so uncoordinated and clumsy. Lucas loved to watch sports, but he'd never been able to play them well. He beamed with pride whenever he watched Noah compete, vicariously living through him.

I enjoyed watching him too and I didn't even like sports, but everyone loved to watch Noah swim. He started drawing crowds in middle school because of the way he possessed the water. It was like he understood it in a way nobody else did. There was never any hesitation in his movements. His long and lean body moved through the water with fluidity and grace. His movements were precise, stroke after stroke executed to perfection. I couldn't help but wonder if I'd ever sit in the bleachers again and cheer for him as he finished a race.

I lined his trophies on the shelf I hung yesterday and arranged the ribbons from his track meets on the pegs below. The ribbons were mostly blue with only a few red and green tails peeking out because even though swimming was his best sport, he was a gifted runner too. The hundreds of hours he spent swimming gave him incredible endurance and he'd been running varsity track since eighth grade, leading their distance relay team to a state championship title two years in a row. I fingered his ribbons, whispering a silent prayer to a God I didn't know if I believed in anymore that he'd find his way back to the sports he used to love.

I untangled the cords from his PlayStation, wondering whether I should figure out how to hook it up or leave it in the box. His probation forbade Internet use, and I didn't know if it required a connection to work, but I was pretty sure it did. What would he do without his video games? They unwound him after school or any other time he was stressed. I tucked the console in the back of his closet and stacked his games next to it because he didn't need another reminder of something he'd lost staring him in the face every day.

I made and remade his bed, trying to make it look perfect, but it didn't look right. His old red comforter lined with navy-blue stripes seemed juvenile and out of place in his new room. It no longer fit. I wanted to buy him a new comforter, but couldn't afford it until after I got paid next Friday. It had taken me a long time to learn how to live paycheck to paycheck since I hadn't had to do it since early in my marriage. It felt weird to be working again even though it had been nine months. I was forced to go back to work to help pay for Noah's rehabilitation because all of our accounts were drained on lawyer costs and court fees. Treatment was court-ordered, but the family was responsible for paying part of the cost and it wasn't cheap.

I worked full-time as a nurse at Providence Hospital prior to Noah being born, but had been a stay-at-home mom ever since. I loved being a nurse, but as soon as the pregnancy stick showed two red lines, I started planning my career as a stay-at-home mom. I'd always wanted to be a mom. I grew up playing house and secretly played with dolls long after my other friends had given them up.

The day I found out I was pregnant was one of the happiest

days of my life. Lots of women complained about having to stay at home and take care of their kids or how much they missed their jobs and old life, but I never did even when it was hard. I cherished being the most important caregiver in my children's lives and couldn't imagine giving them to someone else to raise while I went to work. I got to be the one who gave them their first bites of solid food and clap when they took their first steps rather than having to hear about it secondhand from someone else. I wanted to know my children better than anyone, and it was impossible to be that close when you only saw them for a few hours a day.

As the bills and past-due notices piled up, Lucas started hinting it was time for me to go back to work. His hints grew into demands the higher the numbers climbed, but I couldn't bring myself to go back to work at the hospital because of the effect it would have on Katie. I wanted to be home with her and as involved in her life as I'd been with Noah. I got lucky and found a job as a medical transcriptionist that allowed me to work from home. It didn't pay nearly as much as nursing, but it was enough to offset the bills and keep us afloat.

I wandered into my bedroom. Noah had all his furniture from his old room, but I didn't have any. I couldn't justify buying a new bedroom set for a temporary situation. If things went as planned, we would only be in the apartment for a year until he went to college, and I could sacrifice until then. My bed was the blow-up air mattress we used on camping trips with an extra comforter thrown over it. My clothes were folded in hanging organizers in the closet since I didn't have a dresser.

For a moment, I allowed myself to remember what our home

used to be like, something I rarely let myself do because it made me so sad. My life was forever divided into a distinct before-and-after sequence. I hated this new life, but I loved my life before in Buffalo Grove, back when I was living my happily ever after and had everything I wanted—a devoted husband, two healthy, adorable children, and a life centered on taking care of them.

Lucas and I met the summer of my freshman year in college while we were building a house for Habitat for Humanity. He was the project manager, and we worked side by side for weeks before he talked to me about something other than construction. I was surprised to discover he'd grown up a few hours south of the small town in Wisconsin where I spent my childhood. Most of the volunteers came from all over the country and since we were the only two locals, we bonded over our shared Midwestern upbringing and being the only children in our families. Our relationship developed slowly and as the summer went on I started wondering if he was ever going to ask me out on an official date.

I'd spent all my high school years in a relationship with my childhood sweetheart, whom I'd been sure I was going to marry since I was thirteen. He was a year older than me and broke up with me a week after his high school graduation. He said he wanted to be free to enjoy college life, but I was crushed because I knew it was code for hooking up with other girls. I spent my senior year heartbroken and refusing to date anyone.

I started dating again once I got to college, and it didn't take me long to figure out I hated it. I had no interest in one-night stands or casual dating. It was old-fashioned, but I viewed dating as shopping for my future husband and didn't want to waste time on anyone who wasn't interested in a committed relationship. But

Lucas wasn't like other guys I met. He made references to marriage and having a family all the time. He was focused and driven with no time for any of the distractions college life provided. He was practical and straitlaced, majoring in accounting. Just when I thought I'd been permanently placed in the friend category, he asked me out to dinner.

There weren't any fireworks or starry-eyed looks, but I knew after our first dinner that he was the one. He was like curling up on the couch with a blanket and stepping into my favorite book. We slid into a relationship easily and effortlessly and he brought me home to meet his parents that Christmas. We were engaged within six months. He was as eager to start building a life together as I was.

At the time, we lived in downtown Chicago, but planned to live in the northern suburbs after we got married because we wanted our children to grow up where they could play in the streets and walk to the store to pick up milk by themselves like we did when we were kids. It was important for us to give them the experiences we cherished from our childhood, like running through the neighborhood unencumbered, climbing trees, catching lightning bugs, and having lemonade stands on the sidewalk. A place where police officers were friends and you hailed them down to give you football cards during football season. We both knew the world wasn't a safe place but wanted to protect their innocence for as long as we could.

Buffalo Grove was the perfect spot to raise our family. It was a nice middle-class neighborhood thirty miles outside of Chicago, and we moved as soon as I graduated. Our house was a large split-level at the end of cul-de-sac where all the houses looked the same.

It was a tight-knit community with picturesque tree-lined streets. It was exactly what we wanted with its beautiful homes, safe neighborhoods, and friendly faces. We were close enough to the excitement of the city but far enough away to be insulated from the dangers of it.

I naively thought nobody would find out about what Noah had done because he was the small-town star and everyone loved him. He'd been featured in the local newspaper since he was nine for all the athletic awards he'd won and the attention he'd drawn from scouts at such an early age. People thought he was going to become the next Michael Phelps. Our church raised money through garage sales and car washes to send him to expensive tournaments and hire private coaches we wouldn't have been able to afford otherwise. He wasn't just our son—he was everyone's, so I assumed his troubles would be a private matter we'd work out between our families. I expected the girls' parents to have a measure of understanding and compassion since Noah was a kid and wasn't even at the age of consent himself.

I second-guessed every decision we made after Noah's confession, and telling the parents of the girls wasn't any different. It seemed like the right thing to do at the time. We had no idea the chain reaction it would set off. I would always wonder what would've happened if we'd never had that dinner or had handled things differently, but we didn't, and we could never go back.

I made the decision to tell the parents without any input from Lucas because he was still reeling from Noah's confession. He barely moved and shuffled through the house like someone died. His eyes stricken. He didn't hear me when I talked. My questions were met with blank stares and the sentences he managed to string together were mostly incoherent. I should've given him more time, but I was determined to resolve things quickly, get everyone the help they needed, and move forward with our lives.

It seemed silly now. I looked back on who I was then and couldn't help but feel sorry for myself. I was so clueless. I still believed in compassion and that doing the right thing was rewarded, and telling the girls' parents was the right thing to do even if the way we did it was wrong.

I didn't know either of the parents well. Our kids weren't near enough in age to spend a lot of time together, but both girls went to the same elementary school as Katie. We all attended Sacred Heart, but we went to early mass and they went to the afternoon mass so we only saw them at Christmas and Easter or other special occasions when the entire congregation came together. I couldn't call them up and invite them to dinner without giving them a reason, so I told them we were inviting them over to talk about something that happened during their daughters' swimming class without giving them the specific details. I stressed it was an adults-only dinner. Both mothers pressed me for more information but I dodged their questions and assured them things would be okay once we sat down and talked.

The Johnsons and Williams arrived together, obviously having talked to each other beforehand to time their arrival. The husbands, Jim and Michael, each had a protective arm slung around their wife's waist, gripping them close to their bodies. Normally, we would've had a few drinks in the living room before moving into the dining room for dinner, but nothing about the dinner was normal and we all knew it even though we tried to act casual as I ushered them into the dining room. The mothers, Nora and Cheryl, kept exchanging glances with each other from across the table as I chattered away about the upcoming school play and how I hoped winter would hold off as long as possible. Each couple sat on one side of the table while Lucas and I perched at each end. It was more awkward than any first date I'd been on.

"Can I get you anything to drink?" I asked. The air was thick with tension.

"I'll have some water," Nora's husband, Jim, said.

"Of course. Anyone else?" I prattled off the list of options. Nora stopped me when I got to wine.

"I'll take a glass," she said.

"Me too," Cheryl said, flashing me a nervous smile.

"Can I change my order?" Jim laughed. "Do you have any hard stuff?"

"Absolutely." I motioned to Lucas to follow me into the kitchen. So far, he'd been staring at the framed art on the wall as if it was the first time he'd seen it and not making any effort at small talk to help put them at ease. He hadn't said a word since the formal introductions at the front door.

I pulled out our best wine and bourbon, the ones we reserved for holidays and special occasions. Lucas helped as I fumbled around in the kitchen as if it wasn't mine.

"This is insane," he hissed in my ear.

I handed him the bourbon. "You could be a little more helpful with all this. Maybe if you said something."

"I'm not going to pretend like this is some kind of social event. I just want to get this over with." He grabbed the bourbon, turned, and headed back into the dining room.

I followed, carrying the glasses and wine bottle. I placed them on the table, filling the ladies' glasses with red wine while he filled the men's with bourbon. After he poured their glasses, he lifted the bottle to his lips and took a long pull. I'd never seen him drink straight from the bottle. He shuddered with revulsion, then took another swig. He didn't shudder this time. He wiped his lips with the back of his sleeve.

"Good stuff," he said.

Our eyes were glued to him.

"Honey, why don't you take a seat?" I said with a fake smile plastered on my face.

He cocked his head to the side, and his eyes filled with challenge. For a minute, I thought he was going to remain standing, but he sank into his chair slowly, never taking his eyes off me.

"What's going on here?" Jim asked. He raised his eyebrows and stared at Lucas. Lucas returned his stare with a blank expression on his face.

I stepped in, breaking the awkward stare down. "I'm sorry this is so weird. We wanted to tell you together—"

"Please, just tell us what's going on." Cheryl's newly manicured red nails gripped her husband Michael's arm.

I looked toward Lucas. He shrugged his shoulders and drained what was left in his glass like he was at a fraternity party.

"Lucas and I have talked about it, and we want you to know we're willing to do anything to help your girls and make this right." My voice shook. "All our kids are going to need help to work through this, and it's important we decide together how we want to talk to them about it, what we want to say, and how we'll handle things from here." I looked toward Lucas for help again. This time, he looked away. "We'll pay for both your girls to see a therapist for as long as it takes. Seriously, you don't have to worry about the money."

"What are you talking about?" Jim pushed his chair back from the table, hard enough to make the glasses shake.

"Why would you pay for our kids to see a therapist?" Cheryl asked. Her eyes filled with confusion.

"It's hard to know the right things to say. I don't think any of us have ever dealt with anything like this," I said.

I still thought of us as a team and on the same side. We were a group of parents whose kids had gone through something terrible and would work together to get them through it because we all wanted the same things for them or so I thought. How foolish of me.

Cheryl's eyes narrowed to slits. "What are we dealing with?"

Lucas stared into his glass of bourbon. I wished I was close enough to kick him underneath the table. I swallowed the lump in my throat. My throat was so dry. I picked up my glass of wine and took a sip, hoping it would help. It didn't. I cleared my throat. Cleared it again. "You have such great girls. Noah has really enjoyed working with them. I—"

"Tell us what is going on." Michael's voice was firm, any pretense of a social gathering gone.

I opened my mouth, but nothing came out. I kept trying, but couldn't bring myself to speak the words. Saying it out loud would make it a reality I couldn't take back. Everyone's eyes bored into me.

"Our son molested your daughters during swim practice," Lucas announced.

The room spun and then stilled. Lucas's words hung in the air. Nobody spoke. At first, nobody moved. Jim unfroze first and started looking behind him and leaning forward to peek out into the hallway as if he was waiting for someone to come in with a video camera and tell him it was a joke. Nora sat next to him with a strange smile stuck on her face and stared at Lucas without blinking. Cheryl jerked on Michael's arm, trying to get him to snap out of his shock, begging him to do something.

Lucas stood and pushed in his chair. "I'm sorry. Like Adrianne said, we'll do whatever we can to help your girls. Pay for their counseling. Anything." His shoulders sagged and he hung his head. "Sorry."

He grabbed the bottle from the table and walked out of the room while we stared at his back. Where was he going? What was he doing? The front door opened and then closed, followed by the sound of his car starting. I frantically looked around the room, searching for the right thing to say as if the secret was written on the wall somewhere.

"We're leaving too." Michael reached down and pulled Cheryl up from her chair. She leaned against him for support, and he helped her walk to the door. She looked like she might fall over if he didn't. I trailed after them, mumbling apologies.

"Stay away from us," she said as they reached the doorway, not bothering to get their coats. He pushed her through.

Nora and Jim stood behind me in the entryway, staring at me in horror.

"I can imagine what you're thinking right now, and I'm sure it's the worst-case scenario, but I've talked to Noah, and it was pretty innocent stuff. Just kids playing doctor, but he should've known better because he's older. We know that, and he knows that too. He didn't hurt them, not like you think. I know what you're imagining." I talked so fast my words tripped over each other. "I mean, I know it wasn't okay, and I'm sure it was probably confusing for them. Noah's confused too, but kids go through things like this all the time. I think if we talk to them and let them know we're here for them and answer all their questions that they'll be okay. I'm sure they're going to have lots of questions. I'm not an expert, so I have no idea how to answer them, but there's people who are and they can help us."

Even after I stopped talking, Nora kept bobbing her head up and down, her dark hair flopping forward in her face. Jim looked like he wanted to punch something and if Lucas had been there, I was sure he would've.

"So just doctor stuff? Regular kid stuff?" Nora asked.

"Yes, that's all it was. He didn't hurt them—I mean, he hurt them, but not like that, just, stuff. Things he shouldn't have done."

"We need to talk to Maci," Jim said.

"Are you sure? I mean, maybe we don't need to talk to her if Adrianne says it wasn't a big deal. Don't you think she would've said something to us if it was bothering her? She's acting perfectly normal." Her eyes were wide, unblinking.

"Come on. We aren't having this conversation in front of her." He glared at me and pulled Nora toward the door.

I hurried to gather their coats from the closet. They looked at them with disgust like they didn't want anything that had been in our house when I handed them their coats, but they took them anyway. I kept promising we'd get Noah into counseling as I followed them out, assuring them it was a lot for our families to take in all at once, but that we'd be okay and I was sure we could move through it successfully.

I couldn't have been more wrong.

I'd never forget the knock on the door that Sunday morning. I had no idea who would be knocking at our door so early. I hurried to the doorway, tying my lavender robe around me. I peeked through the peephole and saw two uniformed police officers standing on the front porch. Terror seized me.

My immediate thought wasn't of Noah, because I never imagined he'd be arrested. Kids didn't get arrested unless they committed horrible crimes, and I didn't view what he'd done as a crime. I thought someone had died. Had Lucas left without me knowing and been killed in a car accident on the way home? Had something happened to my mom?

"Are you the mother of Noah Coates?" The taller one of the two asked.

I nodded. I couldn't find my voice.

"We're here for your son," he said.

"I don't understand. What's happening?"

"Ma'am, we have a warrant for his arrest."

My gut clenched at the word *arrest*. They burst through the door without waiting for me to invite them in. They stormed up the stairs as if they'd been in my house before. Lucas met them in the hallway in his boxers, his hair sticking up all over his head, still reeking of booze.

"What's going on?" he asked.

"Sir, move out of the way. We're here for your son, Noah." They pushed past him as if he weighed nothing.

I ran to Katie's door and blocked it with my body. I didn't

want them to barge into her room and scare her. I pointed across the hallway. "That's his room."

They shoved open his door without knocking.

"Noah Coates?"

I waited for his voice, but there was only silence. They pulled him through the door, hands behind his back in cuffs with head down, and his long dark curls falling forward on his face. His body was slack, defeated. He didn't look back as they pulled him down the stairs.

"Noah, it's going to be all right. We're going to figure this out," I called after him, following him down the stairs as they read him his rights, my heart pounding in my chest. "I love you. It's going to be okay. I love you, honey."

"You have the right to remain silent. Anything you say can be used against you. You have a right to an attorney..."

Just like that, they were gone. I collapsed in sobs on the foyer floor.

The story leaked throughout town, spreading like wildfire and gaining momentum as it traveled. The case was featured on the local news. They didn't give Noah's name because he was a minor, but it didn't matter. By that time, everyone had heard. The stories stretched further and further from the truth as they traveled from mouth to mouth. At one point, there were rumors he belonged to a cult and had raped everyone in the swim class as part of his initiation.

It was as if we'd been catapulted back to the 1980s and our entire family had AIDS. People were afraid to be in our space or get too close to us like they might catch what we had. They watched us like wolves. They hated Lucas and me as much as Noah because we'd created the monster who hurt their children. The sacred pieces of our beautiful life were stripped from us one by one.

It started with the school. I was secretary of the PTA and received a letter from the president asking me to resign from my position and not attend any of the meetings until further notice. His letter was nice in comparison to the scathing emails I received from the carpool monitor and volunteer coordinator. Venomous hate filled every line. They made it clear I was no longer welcome to participate in any activities with the kids.

We made lots of mistakes in the beginning, and the biggest one was sending Noah to school after he'd been arraigned because we were desperate to return to some form of normalcy. We didn't know normal no longer existed for us, or that the life we knew was gone.

Noah called me at 11:30 on his first morning back.

"Hi, honey. How's it going?" I tried to sound chipper, pretending as if I hadn't been crying since I dropped Katie off.

His voice was barely a whisper. "You have to come get me. Now. I'll meet you in the back parking lot."

"Honey, we talked about this. It's going to be difficult, but you can get through it. It's going to take a while, but—"

"You have to come get me," he hissed.

"I'm sorry, but I can't do that." I wanted to so badly, but knew the importance of not rescuing my kids from their mistakes.

"Mom, please." His voice quivered.

"I said no. I ju—"

"I'm all bloody. You have to come get me."

"What do you mean you're all bloody?"

"Just get here. You'll see."

The call ended.

I raced to the school and pulled into the rear parking lot next to the football field. He limped across the lot with his head down, shoulders slumped, and holding his side. He slid into my car, refusing to look at me.

"Let me see you," I demanded.

"Mom, no," he whimpered.

I reached over and lifted his head.

"Oh my God," I gasped.

Angry purple welts and deep red cuts raked the side of his face as if he'd been dragged. His left eye was swollen shut, and his right one lined in blue. A steady trickle of blood ran from his nose onto his white uniform shirt. His lip bulged, cracked in the middle. I reached out to touch him, and bring him close.

"Don't." He scooted against the door, curling into a ball on the seat.

"What happened?"

He shook his head, grimacing in pain with his movements.

"Please, Noah, tell me what happened. Who did this to you?" I couldn't hide the desperation in my voice.

"It doesn't matter."

I shook my head. "It does matter. Tell me who did this."

"They jumped me in the locker room," he said softly.

"The team?"

Noah was captain of the swim team, and they met for a short practice every day during fourth period.

He nodded.

"All of them?"

He nodded again.

"You stay here. I'm going back inside. I'm going to have a talk with Coach Hunt. This is unacceptable." I reached for my purse.

"Mom, don't, just don't, please."

I shook my head. "This is *not* okay. Coach Hunt won't stand for this kind of behavior."

Noah grabbed my hand with bloodied knuckles. "He was there, Mom. The entire time. He watched from his office window."

I felt as if I'd been slapped. Coach Hunt was like a second father to Noah. He'd been his primary coach since sixth grade and worked with him privately during the summer at the pool in his backyard. We'd had him and his wife over for dinner numerous times over the years. I gripped the wheel, my hands shaking, thoughts whirling.

He never went back to school, and I started homeschooling him while we waited for his trial, but people refused to leave us alone. A group of students and parents marched through town plastering trees and posts with flyers warning: *Beware of this child molester.* His picture was blown up underneath—the same photo posted in the sophomore yearbook where he'd been voted most likely to succeed and the one we'd given the *Courier* after he'd won the Presidential Award for Academic Excellence. There was a phone number for anyone to call if they were one of his victims or had any information about the case. We saw his face everywhere we went.

I couldn't go to the grocery store without everyone staring holes into me. People moved aside when I passed them in the aisles. Some shook their heads. Others pointed at me and whispered to their friends. The cashiers didn't want to take my money as if my bills were contaminated and turned their noses up at me like I smelled foul. One Friday while waiting in line for the bank teller, a woman I recognized from the prison ministry at church turned and asked me if I was Noah's mom. People had stopped speaking to me, so it took me by surprise.

"Y-yes, I am." I felt the red moving to my cheeks.

She took a step toward me. "What are you doing here? You and your family are disgusting." She spat at me, her fluid landing on my forehead, dripping down into my left eye.

The bank was filled with people, and everyone watched. The man in front of the woman patted her on the back like she'd scored the winning point in the championship game. It was impossible to hide my shame and humiliation as the tears stung my eyes. I mumbled apologies as I moved through the crowd, turning this way and that as I skirted through them, running for the door. I didn't even get gas in Buffalo Grove after that and started driving three suburbs away to do my errands.

Lucas was an accountant and he'd built a thriving business over the years. His clients came to him through word of mouth because of the reputation he'd built for being honest and willing to go to any length for them. We never imagined his business would be affected, but his clients started pulling their accounts until even the most loyal were gone. He had no choice but to start looking for work at a new firm in Chicago. He landed a job downtown and had to take a huge pay cut while he built his clientele all over again.

Lucas wanted to move, but I refused. Our house was our sanctuary—every room thoughtfully and lovingly designed, where I'd carried each of my babies home from the hospital, filled with memories of Christmas and holidays, games in the backyard, and home-cooked meals in the kitchen. I desperately hoped people would eventually leave us alone and move on.

My last shred of hope vanished the afternoon we returned from a Cubs game. We'd gone to the game hoping it would provide some relief from the ever-present darkness surrounding us, threatening to devour us whole. It had worked. Noah had even laughed at lunch and spoken more than two words. Katie spotted it first as we stepped out of the car.

"Mom, what's that say?" she asked, pointing at the house.

I looked up to see the words *Baby Raper* spray-painted in black across our front door. I clamped my hand over my mouth. Lucas covered Katie's eyes even though she couldn't read, as if the hideousness of the words could still reach her. I turned toward Noah, hoping he hadn't gotten out of the car and I could create a distraction before he saw it, but it was too late. He stood still as a statue, transfixed on the words marking his childhood home. His eyes filled with unyielding sadness and despair.

We put our house on the market a week later. Three weeks after Noah was locked up, we moved to Dolton, as far south as we could get without crossing over to the proverbial other side of the tracks. Our downtown laced with thriving specialty restaurants, designer clothing boutiques, and seasonal festivals was gone. It'd been replaced with a chicken factory and chemical plant. Our new house was much smaller than our house in Buffalo Grove, but it was all we could afford since Noah's trial drained all our savings and most of our retirement funds. We had to practically give our house away to the only person who made an offer because nobody local would touch it.

We enrolled Katie in kindergarten at the local public school. It was a sharp contrast to the expensive private school they were used to. There were over thirty kids in each classroom. Unlike their old school, where each kid had their own iPad to take home for their homework, there weren't enough textbooks for each child to have one, and they had to share. Their school had been filled with extracurricular activities, but Katie's new school didn't have music, arts, or a physical education teacher. I threw myself into improving the school. It helped to have a project and gave me something to focus on besides Noah.

I organized a group of parents and began hosting monthly meetings in the library. Our meetings had to be in the evenings because unlike Buffalo Grove, most kids came from households where both parents worked. Fundraising was our first priority. We hosted car washes, had bake sales, and sold gift wrap from catalogues. By the end of the year, we'd raised enough money to hire an art teacher to come in once a week the following year.

We'd found anonymity in Dolton. The people were too busy trying to survive to care about anyone else's problems but their own. I hoped our anonymity extended to Noah and gave him the second chance he needed. I desperately wanted the opportunity for a fresh start and to move forward. Not just for him, but for all of us.

HIM(THEN)

I sink my teeth into the blanket to stifle my cries and will myself to breathe. It's been five weeks and nothing has changed. It hasn't gotten any easier. I panic every night when they lock me in and turn down the lights. There's no way to know if there's anyone on the other side of the steel door. There's no windows. No lights. It's like being in a black box. They could leave me here for days if they wanted to, and no one would ever know.

They used to leave the doors unlocked at night but kids snuck into other rooms and beat each other. I heard a rumor someone got killed but I'm not sure if it's true. I never know what to believe around here because people lie just as much as they tell the truth. We used to have roommates but they don't allow that anymore either.

I didn't sleep at all my first week. I couldn't even make myself lay in the bed. I paced back and forth like a caged animal listening to the sounds around me. The old building moaned and creaked all night long. Nobody cries during the day, but everything changes when the lights go out. Some of the kids screamed like they were being tortured, and I was afraid I'd be next. The walls are so thin you can hear everything except if you're in the quiet room. The quiet room is where they send you when you're bad, and you can't hear anything in there.

Ben is in the room on my left, and he falls asleep within minutes. I always know when he's out because he snores so loud. I don't know how he does it. Maybe it's because he's used to being locked up. He's been locked up in over nine different placements. Almost everyone here has been locked up before. They brag about it like it's something to be proud of.

Not me. I'm never coming back. This has to work. It has to fix me. I'm not cut out to live like this. I'm scared all the time. I worry the others will smell my fear, and I've seen what they do to the kids who are afraid. So far I've been left alone, but I'm not sure how much longer it'll last.

I focus on staying out of everyone's way. I don't look people in the eyes. Not even in any of the groups. I stare at the floor, trying to create designs in the carpet. I speak if someone talks to me, but I don't strike up conversations myself. I couldn't even if I wanted to. I don't know how to talk to these kinds of kids. I've never hung out with bad kids, and now I'm surrounded by them. Most of them are proud of what they did, and it makes me sick. I throw up after group when they share their stories about the people they've hurt. I've learned to throw up quietly so no one knows I'm doing it.

Ben isn't one of the bad ones. He wants to be but he's not. He's too nerdy. His face is covered in pimples, and you can see the dandruff in his greasy hair because he never washes it. He hates taking showers, so he always smells like dirty socks. One of his treatment goals is to take a shower every day, but he still refuses. He's my treatment buddy, and I don't say anything about his smell because I'd rather be paired up with someone like him than get stuck with someone like Joe.

Joe terrifies me, but it's not just me. He terrifies everyone, even the counselors. They pretend like they're not scared of him, but they are. I see it in their eyes when they look at him. He came from juvenile prison, where he served four years for burning his grandmother's house down and almost killing her. Half of her body is covered with burns and she lives in a nursing home now because she can't take care of herself. He's been in trouble since he was a toddler. When he was five, his parents brought home a new puppy and he broke all the dog's legs. Just snapped them like twigs. He laughs every time he tells the story. He got locked up for the first time when he was seven because he cut his baby sister with a knife. Sliced her whole arm. He said he did it because he wanted to see what blood looked like. He has to be locked up until he's twenty-one.

Everyone looks up to him like he's some sort of hero or freezes in terror when he comes close. No one wants to piss him off. I've never seen eyes like his. They're like tunnels of darkness. So black. I'm pretty sure he's pure evil.

He gets sent to the quiet room all the time. The walls are padded in there and there's only a small peephole to look out. You have to bang on the door to get let out to go the bathroom and if they don't come, you have no choice but to go in the bucket in the corner. There's a mattress on the floor where you sleep like a dog. I've seen what the kids look like when they come out of there—

manic and wild-eyed—but not Joe. He comes out with a big smile on his face like it didn't faze him in the least.

It's still a shock to my system every morning when I wake up that I'm here. I don't think that part will ever get easier. And as much as I try to convince myself that I'm not as bad as they are, I'm here. I'm locked up with them, and that means I'm one of them.

3

"What do you think?" I asked.

Katie stood in the living room in her pink leotard, clutching her backpack close to her chest as she surveyed the battered couch I got from Goodwill and the old TV with a box behind it despite its flat screen.

"It's okay." It was the closest she could get to lying. She couldn't bring herself to say it looked good, but she cared too much about hurting my feelings to say it looked awful.

I tousled her short hair, cut to a pixie length framing her petite face. She refused to grow her hair long. She said it itched her ears too much.

Last night Lucas and I told her that I would be moving into an apartment with Noah after he gets released. I spent yesterday preparing for the conversation. I researched how to minimize the impact of telling a young child about divorce since it was the only topic that came close to describing our living situation. Everything I read stressed the importance of the parents talking to the child together and making it clear they still loved them. The most critical piece of the conversation was to make sure the child felt loved and understood none of the changes in their living situation were their fault. However, in the context of a real divorce children spent time in each of the households, but Katie wouldn't be spending the night in the apartment with Noah and me. Lucas was against any sleepovers. I emailed him some of the major talking points while he was at work and told him to review them before he got home.

I cooked her favorite dinner, spaghetti and meatballs, hoping it would put her in a good mood. We splurged and had ice cream for dessert, complete with rainbow sprinkles on hers. Lucas and I tumbled over each other with questions about her day and how she was feeling.

"What's going on?" she asked, looking back and forth between us when we moved to the living room. She never missed anything.

"Daddy and I have something we need to talk to you about." I looked toward him. He nodded, and I continued. "Noah is getting out of treatment in three days, and we're going to have to make some changes in our family."

"We want you to know we love you very much." Lucas put his arm around her, squeezing her tightly.

"We love Noah, too. Both of you are the most important things to us," I said.

Her face was expressionless as she waited to hear the next big change in her life.

"Noah isn't going to live in this house when he gets out. Our family is going to have two places to live. Mommy got an apartment for her and Noah. They are going to live in the apartment and you and I are going to live in this house. We'll see each other all the time and spend time together even though we're not going to live together. We're still going to be a family. It's just that our family is going to look different than it did before." His voice was tender.

I wished I believed him. Katie eyed him suspiciously, not believing his words any more than I did. I kissed her on the top of her head. I reminded myself of the importance of maintaining a united front.

"Some of the kids you go to school with live in different houses—"

"But their parents are divorced. Are you guys getting a divorce?" Her pale blue eyes were wet.

"No, of course, not. Daddy and I are still going to be married." I swallowed my fear that she was right, and it was where we were headed when all this was over.

"Then, why are we living in two houses? I don't understand. Why can't Noah come home?" Her lower lip quivered. It was only a matter of time before she crumbled into tears.

I looked at Lucas, directing the question back at him. This was his idea, not mine. I felt the same way she did. Noah was still our family. Nothing changed that.

He cleared his throat, clearly uncomfortable as both our gazes fixed on him, searching for answers. "Katie, there's some things you're too young to understand. Remember how we've talked about the difference between adult and kid issues?"

She nodded her head, the distrust still in her eyes.

"Our decision to live in separate houses is an adult issue. We don't want you to have to worry about it. All you need to know is how much we love you and that none of this is your fault. We're doing the best thing for our family. We have to keep you safe."

"Safe from what?" She turned toward me. "Mommy, what's there to be afraid of?"

I didn't have the strength to tell her. The air hung heavy with her unanswered question. Lucas finally broke the silence. "We need to make sure you're safe from Noah."

"Why would Noah hurt me?" Her face crumpled in confusion.

I fought the urge to cry. I wanted to wrap my arms around her and assure her Noah would never hurt her, tell her that she was right, and there was no reason to be afraid of her big brother. Her hero. I forced myself to be strong for her. I wouldn't cry.

"Noah has made some bad decisions that hurt other people. We have to make sure he doesn't hurt you too," Lucas said.

She shook her head back and forth. "Noah would never hurt me. Ever."

I pulled her onto my lap and wrapped my arms around her. I felt her heart pounding in her back. Her frail body shook. The tears she'd fought so hard against wet my shirt. "I know, sweetie, Noah loves you. He does. He's going to be so sad about this too. I can promise you that." I couldn't help myself and whispered in her ear, hoping Lucas couldn't hear, "You're right. Noah would never hurt you."

Lucas didn't speak to me the rest of the night. We went to bed in what was becoming our usual position—each on our side with our backs facing each other.

"You should've backed me up," he snapped as we made coffee this morning.

"I agree with her."

I couldn't explain how I knew he wouldn't hurt her, but a mother's love was unexplainable and I knew Noah. I did. His heart was good even if I couldn't reconcile it with what he'd done. Lucas glared at me, grabbed his travel mug, and stomped out the door, slamming it behind him. I texted him this afternoon to tell him I was going to take Katie to the apartment after I picked her up from school.

I didn't want her to be scared of Noah. It might be naive, and there were lots of people who might share Lucas's feelings, but his counselors always stressed the importance of loving him despite his mistakes. Besides his counselors and myself, Katie was the only other person who didn't look at him like he was a vile creature. She looked at him with kindness, and he needed that.

"Are you hungry? Can I make you something?" I asked her. I went shopping earlier in the day and stocked up on all of Noah's favorites. I was going to make him my special pancakes every morning for the first week.

"I'm not hungry," she said, shaking her head.

I led her through the rest of the apartment, showing her the bedrooms on each side of the hallway with a bathroom at the end.

She turned up her nose. "You have to share a bathroom with him? He's going to leave all his gross hairs in the sink. Eww!"

I burst out laughing. "Maybe I'll start peeing in a bucket in my room." I grabbed her and tickled her sides. She squealed. I wrestled her into my bedroom, tumbling onto my bed, and cuddled her next to me.

"Your room smells funny," she said, turning up her nose.

"The people who lived here before were smokers. I tried to get the smell out."

"Not funny bad. Just different. I miss our old house."

"The one in Buffalo Grove?"

She nodded.

I was glad she remembered it. One of my biggest fears was that she wouldn't have any memory of when her family was intact or the times we were happy, and our house was filled with laughter. She was too young to remember choosing the paint colors for each room, the games of tag in the backyard, or roasting marshmallows over the fire in the living room during the brutal winters when we longed to be outside again. I talked about them all the time, trying to keep them alive for her. I'd told her about every camping trip we'd taken, and she loved to hear stories about our Disneyland vacation when she was three. I'd told them so many times I'd created the memories for her even if she didn't have any real memory of them.

I held her close, breathing in the scent of her strawberry tear-free shampoo. It was hard to believe I almost passed on the opportunity to have her. It wasn't because I didn't want to have another child, but I didn't think it was possible to love another child as much as I loved Noah.

I fell in love with him instantly, marveling at his perfection and that I'd grown him cell by cell in my body. My feelings stemmed from the deepest parts of me, parts I didn't know existed until I had him. He wasn't a stranger when they placed him in my arms. It was like a missing piece of myself had been returned.

I spent his early days staring at him while he slept. He was one of those perfect babies that other mothers hated. He slept so much I had to tickle his feet to wake him up to eat. He only cried when he was hungry and was easily soothed unlike other horror stories I heard. I'd stare at his tiny clasped fingers that he always kept close to his chest, marveling at how tiny they were. I knew every part of him, from the way he smelled to the way he snorted as he was falling asleep. He was my heart, living and breathing outside my body. I always felt guilty when other mothers complained about how difficult the first months were while I was in a state of bliss and more in love than I'd ever been.

I didn't care what other people said. He wasn't born bad. He was born beautiful and perfect. I could picture him at every age. He inherited Lucas's build, so he was off the growth charts from birth. He was a roly-poly baby with dimples in both cheeks. His giggle lit up the room, and strangers stopped to smile at him. At two, he climbed everything in our house, from the refrigerator to the desk in Lucas's office. We used to joke that he had suction cups on his fingers because of all the times we'd find him splayed out, hanging like Spider-Man from pieces of our furniture. As a toddler, he picked flowers for me on his walks and brought them home to put in a vase on the table. He drew pictures of hearts with Lucas and me inside of them in kindergarten. I could see his toothless grin that lasted through second grade until his teeth finally grew in. Teeth that required braces when he was twelve to straighten out. Unlike other tweens, he went along easily with the braces, making fun of himself by calling himself metal mouth.

"I've never loved a single thing in my life more than you," I wrote in his baby book the day I brought him home from the hospital. By the time he was seven, I'd written it over a hundred times and said it just as many.

It was why I'd waited so long to have a second child. I didn't think it'd be fair to relegate another child to second place. I shared my fears with Lucas, and he laughed at me. He told me I was being ridiculous, that I was born to be a mother, and it was selfish to spend all my love on one child when I had so much to give. I eventually agreed to have another child but secretly harbored my fears throughout my pregnancy.

I didn't know it was possible that I had more love to give, but I did. All my fears disappeared after Katie was born. My heart swelled and expanded. I fell in love with her in the same way I'd fallen for Noah.

She fit right into our home, and Noah was never jealous. All of us doted on her together, marveling at each new thing she did and every milestone she met. Noah used to jump in the car when I picked him up from school and the first thing he'd ask was, "Did she do anything new today?"

He helped me create her baby book and scribbled letters to her right along with me. In preschool when they asked what she wanted to be when she grew up, she said Noah, and she begged to bring him as her date on tea party day. Despite being a teenager, he went along happily. None of us could say no to her.

Katie spent the night in the new apartment with me. We popped popcorn and watched *Charlotte's Web* even though we knew most of the lines by heart. She cuddled up next to me, and I rubbed her back in circles until she fell asleep. How was I going to live a year without seeing her every day?

I'd lived eighteen months separated from my first child, and now I was going to have to spend a year apart from my second. It wasn't fair. Things like this weren't supposed to happen to families like ours. Not when you did everything right. We lived in a nice neighborhood and sent them to the best private schools in the state. We took them to mass every Sunday. We prayed before every meal and each night before they went to bed. We took family vacations and camping trips. We still had family game nights.

How was it possible that this happened to us? I considered praying, but decided against it. If someone would've asked me two years ago if I believed in God, I wouldn't have thought twice about my yes. But I wasn't sure anymore. I hadn't been sure about anything in a long time. If you did everything right and it still turned out wrong, then what was the point?

4

Time crawled as I made the four-hour drive to Marsh on the day of his release. I couldn't help but remember the first time I made the drive, back when I was still reeling from his conviction and unable to wrap my brain around everything that had happened. His arrest went far beyond anything we'd ever imagined having to deal with, and we needed someone to help us navigate the legal minefield, so the first step was finding a lawyer.

There wasn't anyone in Buffalo Grove willing to take our case. I scoured LinkedIn profiles for someone specializing in defending juveniles for sex crimes. Most of the top-notch lawyers were ones who only defended high-profile cases and whose fees far exceeded anything we could pay. I finally found a semiretired lawyer, Meryl, who lived in the northern part of the state. He'd worked sex crimes for years in downtown Chicago and agreed to take on our case for a fifteen-thousand-dollar retainer fee.

My biggest concern was keeping Noah out of jail. He'd already spent one night in jail, and I couldn't stomach the idea of him spending another. They'd kept him in an isolated cell away from the other inmates until his arraignment because of his age. I watched as they led him into court in handcuffs with his head hung low and hair falling forward on his face in the same way they'd taken him out of our house. He sat slumped in the metal chair, defeated and despondent as the formalities of his bail were discussed. They released him on his own recognizance because he was a juvenile and didn't have a criminal record or outstanding warrants.

I'd expected him to be relieved to see me, but he was seething with anger when he got in the car. He slammed the door behind him.

"How could you do that?" he asked.

"What are you talking about?"

"That," he spat and pointed behind him toward the courthouse. "That lawyer."

"I know he doesn't look like your typical lawyer, but you've got to cut him some slack. I just found him last night."

I couldn't blame him for being upset. I'd been shocked by Meryl's appearance too. He'd arrived at four in the morning reeking of old booze and smelling like he hadn't showered for days. He'd sworn there was nothing to the arraignment, and he'd be put together in a few days. I offered him our shower, but despite the shower, he still looked unkempt. He hadn't shaved in days and stubble covered his chin. His hair was unruly and in desperate need of a haircut. I'd expected him to put on a suit, but instead, he showed up at the courthouse in jeans and a flannel shirt.

"He told them I wasn't guilty. Why'd you let him do that? I'm guilty. I did it. I'm not going to say I didn't." His eyes flashed with anger.

I didn't know what was going on or how to proceed. I'd never even had a speeding ticket. Meryl told Lucas and me an arraignment was only a legal formality to get him released, and almost everyone pleaded not guilty. I didn't know if there were options other than what he'd presented us with. I trusted his advice because it was what we paid him for.

"The next time we go to court I'm telling the judge I'm guilty. I don't care what that stupid lawyer says," he said.

I reached over and took his hand, keeping my other hand on the wheel. "Honey, I know none of this makes sense, and it's really scary. I'm scared too. I have no idea what's going on or how any of this works. My only concern for the last twenty-four hours has been finding a lawyer to help us. I didn't think any further than that. I just wanted to get you out of jail."

He looked up at me. Dark bags circled his tear-filled eyes. "You should've just left me there. I deserve to be locked up. They need to put me in jail and throw away the key."

I took a left and pulled over on the side of the road, putting the car in park. "Come here." I reached for him, but he pulled away.

"Don't. Don't touch me." His face was pinched.

I grabbed him and pulled him close to me, wrapping my arms around him. His body was stiff and rigid. He tried to push me away again, but I refused to let him go. "I love you no matter what," I said as I kissed the top of his head. "We'll get through this. You're going to be okay."

Gut-wrenching sobs shook his body. I held him as wave after

wave of despair passed through him. I ran my hand through his hair as he cried until he went limp in my arms. I lifted his head up. I tucked his thick hair behind his ears, smoothed the tears from his cheeks, and wiped his snot with the back of my shirt. I'd never seen so much pain in his eyes.

"Listen, we're going to figure this out. We are. I promise." I rubbed his back as his sobs trailed off into hiccups. "Your dad is taking Katie to Grandma's for a while, so the house is quiet. I'm sure you didn't sleep at all last night, so why don't you take a nap when we get home, and I'll make you something to eat after you wake up? Meryl is coming by the house later tonight to meet with us, and you can ask him whatever you need to ask. But for now, we're going to focus on the next step in front of us, and that's getting home and getting you some sleep. Okay?"

He nodded. His sobs had subsided, but his face was still lined with grief.

"Okay. We can do this." I wasn't sure if I was reassuring him or myself.

*****

Later that evening after Katie was in bed, we sat around the kitchen table with Meryl—the same Formica table where we'd spent hours playing Monopoly, where the kids did their homework, and where countless science projects had been created.

"I'm guilty. I'm not going to lie and say I'm not." Noah glared at Meryl from across the table before he had a chance to speak. Noah had lain down when he got home but didn't look any more rested than he had before. I'd tried to get him to shower before

Meryl arrived but he refused.

"Whoa, slow down there, kiddo. I'm not out to get you. I'm here to help you," Meryl said. He was still in the same jeans and flannel shirt that he'd worn to court but I was happy he'd finally shaved. It made him look a little more put together.

"I don't need your help," Noah said.

I looked at Lucas for support, communicating with my eyes the way married couples do that I wanted him to step in. He looked right through me as if he wasn't seeing me. He'd barely spoken since Noah's arrest and drifted through the house like he was sleepwalking.

Meryl raised his eyebrows. "I beg to differ. I'm thinking about your future. Do you know what would've happened if you'd pleaded guilty this morning?"

"Yes, I'd go to jail where I belong." Noah crossed his arms on his chest.

Meryl shook his head. "Nope. They would've released you either way until your sentencing hearing. What you would've done today is sealed your fate in the adult correctional system because you were in adult court, and if you enter a plea in adult court, the option to try you in juvenile court disappears. And you, my friend, are a juvenile." He smiled at Noah, trying to break the ice, but his smile had no effect. He cleared his throat before continuing. "Our first order of business is to get your case handled by juvenile corrections rather than adult corrections."

"What's the difference?" I asked.

He breathed over his mug, trying to cool the tea I'd prepared. "There's a huge difference. If he's tried as an adult, he has a felony record for the rest of his life, so he'll always have a criminal record even after he gets off the registry. But if he's tried as a juvenile and his case is handled in juvenile court, the state of Illinois will still require him to register as a sex offender, but his felony isn't going to show up on his record for the rest of his life. It'll be gone because juvenile records are sealed. That doesn't happen with adult crimes. Second and most importantly, we have a much greater chance at rehabilitation if he's tried as a juvenile versus an adult. The kid needs treatment, not jail. That's what we'll argue. Any of this making sense?"

Noah looked sheepish. I felt relieved. For the first time in days, some of the tension in my neck dissipated.

"There's other options besides jail?" I asked.

"Absolutely. Lots of them. His life doesn't have to be over."

"I want to go to jail," Noah said with fiery determination in his eyes.

His desire to be punished broke my heart.

"If you go to jail, you're not going to get the help you need. Do you hear what he's saying? There's help out there. You can get help for his," I said.

"Let him go to jail if he wants to," Lucas spoke for the first time.

I snapped my head in his direction. "Did you not hear what Meryl said? We can get him help."

Lucas shrugged his shoulders like he didn't care. I wanted to slap him. How could he think of sending our son to jail rather than getting him the help he needed? I turned to face Noah. His fight had left him. His slump was back.

"Listen, we can plead guilty if that's what you want." Meryl leaned forward across the table to get closer to Noah. "I'm just trying to help you not ruin your life over the whole ordeal. You seem like a good kid."

Did he really believe he was a good kid or was he just saying that because it was his job to pretend like he did? I hoped it was true. Noah needed someone to fight for him besides just me.

It took more convincing, but Noah finally agreed to do what Meryl suggested. I had expected the next part to be easy but was shocked at how hard it was to get Noah tried in juvenile court. The Williams and Johnsons were adamant that he be tried as an adult. They hired a ruthless lawyer who pointed his finger at Noah and yelled, "He's committed a heinous crime against innocent children. Look at the depraved nature of what he's done. We must take his actions seriously and hold him accountable by the strictest court of law."

He went on to argue that Noah knew right from wrong, intended to harm the girls, and was considered a threat to society. "This is not something he did just once. He touched those girls again. And again. And again." He inserted a long, dramatic pause after each *again.* "We aren't just looking out for these girls' lives. We have to keep other children safe from him too. It's in the best interests of the public that we charge him as an adult."

A rush of anger surged through me. How could we apply adult consequences to someone who was so young? Even if he was fifteen, he was still a child. He hadn't started shaving yet and even though his voice was beginning to change, it still slipped into the high-pitched frequency of a child.

Meryl countered by saying it would be cruel and unusual punishment to send him into the adult correctional facility. He cited case after case of children who were raped in adult prisons or committed suicide while they were incarcerated. "Noah is a good kid. He's never been in any trouble with the law. He hasn't spent a day in detention at school. He's an upstanding member of the community already."

He went on to read a list of praise he'd received from his teachers over the years. Things like, "he's one of the best students I've had, he's always willing to help his fellow students, and he's a delight to have in class."

The biggest point he drove home again and again was how Noah had confessed on his own and hadn't hidden anything. He argued it spoke to his true character and showed his remorse, but more importantly, his desire to seek help for what he'd done. "This young boy is the reason juvenile court exists. He is a prime candidate for rehabilitation. Throwing him into an adult jail would be like throwing a kitten into a pack of wolves."

I held back the urge to clap.

Noah didn't speak throughout the entire process. He sat still as stone at the defense table never lifting his head. He looked so small in the vast courtroom. Lucas and I sat behind him on cold wooden benches. I clung to Lucas's hand so tightly my knuckles turned white. Every word reverberated throughout the empty room.

Each of the parents spoke, and they had no mercy. The mothers wept, and the fathers raged. They wanted him tried as an adult and punished in the same manner. Each time they called him a sexual offender, the word cut through my brain like shards of glass.

In the end, the judge conceded, and Noah was adjudicated as a juvenile. The trial was easy in comparison to the pretrial. Noah got his chance to speak and pleaded guilty to four counts of second-degree sexual assault against minors. I clasped my hands together on my lap while the judge handed down his sentence based on the plea bargain the lawyers had worked out. He had to complete eighteen months in a juvenile sex offender program. He would be on probation until he was eighteen and register as a Type I offender, which carried a mandatory ten years on the register. The conditions of his probation were extensive—no contact with anyone under the age of twelve, no contact with his victims, no Internet use in his home, he couldn't live within a mile of an elementary school, no drugs or alcohol use, no pornography, and on and on the list of nos went.

I drove him to the Marsh Foundation the following week. The Foundation sat at the end of a winding one-lane road off Interstate 94. It was a beautiful country home tucked between two acres of forest land on each side. Massive limestone edified the sprawling estate. It looked inviting and tranquil, like a country home for respite, but the sign on the door revealed its true mission: *A rehabilitation center for juvenile sexual offenders.*

We knocked and waited for what seemed like forever before someone answered. Finally, a woman dressed in impeccable business attire opened the door.

"Are you Noah?" Her eyes were friendly as they moved over us.

Noah refused to look up, staring at the pavement underneath our feet. He nodded his head.

"Welcome." She smiled at him and ushered us inside. "You must be Adrianne. I'm Dr. Park. I'm the chief psychologist on the unit." She stuck out her hand to me. Her grip was firm and confident. She was tall and lean with calves peeking out from underneath her blue pencil skirt that you only got from spending hours in the gym each week. Her shiny black hair was cut in a neat bob, framing her face, and tucked behind her ears.

I expected Marsh to look like a jail and was surprised at the warm reception area. It was a small room filled with two sets of chairs on each side and a metal door behind them. Throw pillows lined a brown coach at the back of the room. Noah was visibly shaken and his eyes flicked to the artwork on the walls—ocean beaches and inspirational quotes.

"Unfortunately, I won't be able to provide you with a tour today. Our policy only allows tours on family day, but the good news is our next family day is coming up in two weeks. I hope both you and your husband will be able to attend." She smiled wide, revealing straight teeth that were too white to be natural. "One of our resident counselors will take him to his room and get him settled. How does that sound, Noah?"

He mumbled a reply neither of us could hear.

She placed her hand on his shoulder. "It's okay to be nervous."

He stood frozen to his spot as the metal door opened behind him and a large muscular man walked through. He wore a tight t-shirt outlining every angular cut, and biceps bulged from the sleeves. He nodded at Noah and bent to pick up the duffel bag we'd packed the night before.

My hands were shaking, and I clung to my purse straps to steady them. The longest I'd ever been away from him was for two days when he went on overnight trips with the swim team. How I was going to leave him alone in a building of sex offenders with kids who'd probably committed far worse crimes than him? Would predators devour him at night and steal his last shred of innocence?

"Alan will take him to his room. You'll have to say your goodbyes here," Dr. Park said.

I pulled him close, fighting the urge to grab him and run out the door, to keep running until we'd put all of this behind us and could start over. I breathed in his scent, no longer that of a little boy, but one of body odor and strange teenage smells. His body shook against mine, but his eyes remained dry.

"You're going to get through this. It's going to be okay," I said.

"I love you, Mom," he whispered.

"I love you, too, honey. So much."

The bouncer-looking man peeled him off me and led him through the locked doors. Noah threw a frightened look over his shoulder before it clicked shut behind him. Just like that, he was gone. My resolve crumbled and I let go of the sobs I'd been holding inside.

"It's okay," Dr. Park said in a soothing voice.

I stood there, becoming unhinged, no longer able to deny what was happening. She led me over to one of the chairs, and I collapsed into it, covering my face with my hands.

"He seems like a lovely boy," she said, which only made me sob harder. "I know this is difficult. It's one of the toughest things a parent can go through, but I promise that you're not alone. He's in good hands. We've got one of the best programs in the country."

I'd read everything about their program on their website and from what I'd read, it was true. Their program was rigorous and aimed at decreasing the likelihood of reoffending. They focused on developing positive skills and social interactions, family reunification, and integration back into the community through individual and group therapy, psychoeducation, empathy training, and behavior management. It was all so technical and I didn't understand what half of it meant, but it definitely sounded like they knew what they were doing.

"His life isn't over even though I know it feels like it is. He can go on to have a happy, productive life." Her eyes were kind and soft.

She was the first person who talked about Noah like he was still a person. No one looked at him like a person anymore. I wanted to hug her.

"How?" I asked.

She handed me a box of Kleenex, and I blew my nose, stuffing a few extra in my purse just in case. "There are so many misconceptions about juvenile sex offenders. The most common is that they're like adult sex offenders, but that couldn't be further from the truth. They aren't miniature adults. There's not a lot of evidence showing that they go on to offend as adults. The truth is, relatively few juveniles go on to commit other crimes. The recidivism rate is low."

"Are you sure?"

"Absolutely." She nodded her head with conviction. "We have an even lower recidivism rate than most. Less than three percent of our patients go on to reoffend." Her voice was calm and even, steadying the beat of my pounding heart. "Youth are more changeable than adults. The majority are amenable and benefit from treatment. Boys going through puberty have a surge of hormones that can be difficult to control. They're curious about girls, and sometimes they make bad choices. They don't understand the long-term consequences of their actions. We help them make better choices in the future."

It was what I'd been saying all along. I wished Lucas was there with me to hear an expert say our son wasn't doomed or inherently flawed. He'd made a mistake. A mistake that could be corrected with proper treatment.

"Juveniles and adults aren't the same, so we can't treat them like they are. Noah's brain is still developing. It hasn't had a chance to develop a deviant sexual response system. One of our primary goals of treatment is to work on creating healthy sexual responses."

"Was he abused? Is that what made him this way?" It was awful and I would never admit it to anyone else, but I wanted Noah to have been sexually abused. It would've provided a reason for him doing what he'd done and made sense of something so senseless.

She shook her head. "That's another common misconception. Most sexual offenders haven't been sexually abused. There are a few that have, and of course, we'll assess whether Noah has, but the likelihood that he's been sexually abused isn't great."

"Then why?"

It was the question that kept me up at night. How could I have lived with him for so many years and never had any idea something was wrong with him? I'd wracked my brain for any clue I might have missed, any sign I might not have seen or might have dismissed, but there was nothing there. He'd never harmed another human being. He didn't even let us kill bugs when he was a kid. We had to trap spiders in the house and release them outside. I had to smash flies when he wasn't looking because he cried one time when he saw me do it. He was delicate and gentle with Katie. He blew on her scraped knees to take away the sting of her pain before applying antiseptic. He slept on her floor after she'd gotten freaked out by the monkey in *Toy Story* and was scared of it coming into her room. How could someone who hated suffering hurt other people?

"There's not a single factor we can point to as being solely responsible for the development of deviant sexual responses. It tends to be a combination of factors that contribute to sexual offenses in juveniles."

"What are some of the factors?" I held my breath, hoping she had new information to give me.

"They tend to be socially isolated from their peers and have problems forming friendships with their peers. Most suffer from learning disabilities or struggle academically. Many of them have substance abuse problems or live in homes where there's substance abuse problems."

My heart sank as she rattled off the list of factors I'd read numerous times. None of the criteria described Noah. Not even a little. Noah had more friends than he knew what to do with. Always had. I used to joke he had more of a social life than I did. He was one of those people with a magnetic personality who drew others to him without trying.

The idea of him having a learning disability or problems with academics couldn't have been further from the truth. His teachers had suggested moving him up when he was in second grade because of his giftedness, but Lucas and I decided against it. He'd been with the same group of friends since preschool, and we didn't want him to give them up. Instead, his teachers gave him extra work focused on more advanced thinking skills to keep him excited and engaged in learning. Once he reached high school, he'd been in all honor classes. He'd never gotten anything below an A–.

"Are there problems at home?" she asked.

Her question was inevitable. I wasn't upset she asked. I wondered what went on at home whenever I heard about a kid getting into trouble too. Everyone did. Last year when kids were starting fires on the athletic field, and they finally found the group of teenagers responsible for it, my first thought had been, what was it like for them at home? We blamed parents for children's mistakes. It was that simple.

I didn't fault people for thinking there was something wrong with our family. I would've thought the same thing, but I wished they'd been in our home before our lives changed. Back when I could answer her question with a definitive no. Our family was a safe place. We worked hard at providing a place for our kids where they were nurtured, loved, and respected. We did our best not to raise our voices and apologized when we did. We'd never hit our kids. Not once. Or each other. The only problems in our home started after Noah's confession.

It didn't take Dr. Park long to figure out Noah didn't fit the typical profile. He was unlike the other kids he was institutionalized with, and it became apparent almost immediately. Most kids struggled to conform to the rules and spent the first month balking against the restrictions placed on them, but not Noah. He was the perfect client. He learned the rules and followed them. He stayed within their guidelines. Each boy was assigned a job, and his first job was kitchen duty, where he was responsible for washing the dishes of all thirty-two boys. He never complained and took pride in cleaning up after meals. During recreation time, the others were continually getting into fights with each other, but Noah remained off to the sidelines refusing to participate. He was often the one breaking up the fights. I checked in regularly with Dr. Park on his progress, and as time went on, I could tell she was finding herself faced with the same dilemma as me: how did a boy who seemed so good do something so bad?

As I pulled into the long, familiar driveway, I replayed our last conversation, the one where she told me she'd never had a teen who was so easy to work with, but there was a hesitation in her voice that hadn't been there before as she told me about his final request—he'd asked to write a letter to the girls apologizing for what he'd done. I was surprised she didn't think it was a good idea.

"I'm not sure I agree." It was strange for me to disagree with her since we rarely disagreed. She'd grown to become my only ally when it came to Noah. "Maybe it would be good for him. It might bring him closure. It might even bring the girls closure."

I could hear the doubt in her voice. "Yes, it's good that he's remorseful. He's always been apologetic. He's never had a problem admitting what he did was wrong. I'm just concerned he wants to contact his victims after all this time."

"He's sorry. What's wrong with that?"

"His victims are eight years old."

I still didn't understand. I wished we were having the conversation face-to-face. I couldn't read her over the phone.

"Tell me what you're getting at," I said.

"I'd feel more comfortable if he was concerned about getting out of treatment and all the changes about to take place. His focus should be on how he's going to integrate himself back into life. Not on having contact with his victims. Besides, his probation specifically states he's not to have any contact with his victims, and he knows that."

"It's a letter. He just wants to write them a letter."

"It's a bad idea."

"Why?" I didn't like how she wouldn't come right out and say what she was thinking.

"Noah has made a great client. You know that. We talk about it all the time, but there haven't been any battles. None. It's almost been too easy. I'm wondering if we missed something."

"Missed something? What does that mean? What's wrong with being a good client? What'd he say when you told him that it wasn't a good idea?"

"He said okay and agreed not to write the letter, but I'm not sure he understood why it wasn't a good idea."

"Of course, he didn't. I don't understand either," I snapped.

"You really don't understand?"

"He's sorry. He's spent hours going to empathy training. How many exercises have you gone through in group therapy about the importance of being able to recognize other people's feelings and how your actions hurt others? He's doing exactly what you asked of him."

She let out a deep sigh. "That's just it. He doesn't understand contacting them would cause them more damage. I'm afraid there's another reason he wants to talk to them."

My head spun. How could she have spent so much time praising his progress and raving about what an exemplary client he was and days before his release plant a seed of doubt that there was something wrong with him? That he hadn't been fixed? It was cruel and unfair.

"I'll be there at three on Friday to pick him up. Please have his things ready."

"Adrianne, please don't be upset. I just—"

"I don't want to hear it. He's done his time, everything you and the courts have asked of him. You're the one who told me all he had to do was follow your treatment protocol, and he'd get better. That's exactly what he did. He went above and beyond what you asked him to do. I won't sit here now and listen to you tell me you might've missed something."

"He's a good kid. He is. I'm not saying that. But even good kids—"

"Stop. I'm not listening to you anymore."

I hung up on her and hadn't spoken to her since. She'd left a few messages since then asking me to call her back, but I ignored them. Her betrayal hurt. She promised treatment would help. She gave me a false sense of security that once this was over we could put it behind us. She promised a new life and a new beginning. It was posted on all their pamphlets. How could she wait until the last few days and then drop a bomb on me? I wouldn't have any of it. He was better. He had to be.

HIM(THEN)

I stare straight ahead at the dirty wall in front of me. The cold water pelts my body. Today I don't even care that the water's cold. My body is already shaking because he's coming. I can feel it. You can't get away with what Sam did on the yard. I hate the yard almost as much as I hate the shower because the guards relax and don't pay as much attention to what's going on. Bad things happen when they're not watching.

And something bad is going to happen. The air is charged with it. The others have filed in around me and taken up their spots in the trough, all of us in a straight line underneath our assigned spout. Staff tries to pretend like the small dividers give us some privacy but it's a joke. They're only waist-high and you can still see everything if you look. I try not to think about the filth squishing underneath my feet.

We only get seven minutes in the shower, and I'm counting down the minutes until it's over. Maybe I'll get lucky and won't be here when it happens. I'm on 362 seconds when I hear his voice. It's impossible to miss. He's laughing and joking with the guard at the door. The guards like Joe for some reason. It's not his shower time but they let him in anyway. My stomach drops to my knees. Everything stills.

I hear the smack first. Then, the cry. I clench my teeth.

"Please, Joe. I'm sorry. I didn't mean it," Sam cries from two stalls down.

Sam is new and hasn't even been here two weeks, but he still should've known better than to piss off Joe. Laughing with Joe is okay. Laughing at him is unacceptable. Everyone knows that, so when Sam laughed at Joe after he missed a shot on the basketball court, we all froze, expecting him to do something, but instead he just smacked him playfully and walked away. But I knew it wasn't over.

"Shut the fuck up." Joe's voice is a deep growl. "Bend over."

My lunch heaves into my throat and I force it back down. The vomit leaves a horrid taste in my mouth. I stare at the murky tiles in front of me, counting them up and dividing them by three. Anything to keep me from hearing. Stop me from seeing. I made the mistake of looking once and I'll never be able to erase the image from my mind. It's permanently burned in my brain.

Sam whimpers like a kitten. It's painful to hear but I'm glad he's not screaming. I hate when they scream. It's over quickly and Joe pads back through the shower.

"Don't you worry about what you heard and don't even think about saying shit," he says from behind me. He slaps me on my bare ass before heading back out, passing the guard something as he leaves.

Sam cries. His sobs reverberate off the walls. Nobody moves. Nobody speaks.

Sixty-four seconds. The water turns off.

5

He was quiet on the drive while I chattered on, trying to fill the silence. I flipped through my iPod, trying to find something to make him tap his fingers on his leg like he used to, but nothing grabbed him. He stared out the window as the barren trees passed by. I hated that he was getting out on the brink of winter, right after everything had died and was about to be covered in snow for months. It made his release feel ominous and dreary rather than light and hopeful like I wanted it to be. I wished he'd been released in the summer, and I tried not to think about how we'd make it through the winter months.

"Do you want to stop at Wood Ranch for something to eat?" I asked. Wood Ranch had been a family favorite for years. It was our go-to spot after swim meets because they had the best barbeque in town.

He shook his head.

"That's okay. You're probably right. I'm sure you just want to get home."

He shrugged his shoulders.

I looked at him out of the corner of my eye. Even though it'd been over a year, I still wasn't used to seeing him with short hair. He'd worn it long since he was a toddler, but they cut everyone's hair at Marsh in the same buzz cut like they were all in the army. It made his head look too big for his body. He grew taller every time I saw him and today was no different. He'd grown another inch, but he carried himself like he wasn't sure what to do with his long limbs. He no longer held the strong, confident muscles of an athlete. He was lanky, awkward, and hunched over. His face showed the battle fatigue of what he'd been through. I longed for the smile that used to easily light up his face, but his full lips that used to curve into his trademarked mischievous grin were set in a straight line.

I took a deep breath reminding myself like I'd been doing all day that it was going to take time. I couldn't expect him to go back to the person he was before any more than I could expect myself to go back to the person I was. Those people no longer existed.

"Katie's so excited to see you. It's all she's been talking about all week. She wanted to come see you tonight, but I told her you'd probably be too tired. I promised her she could come spend the day with us tomorrow."

"What about Dad?"

It was the first time he'd asked about him in months. He stopped questioning why he wasn't coming to the visits, and I quit making excuses, but his quiet exit wasn't lost on Noah.

"I'm not sure if he's coming," I said.

He put his hand on my leg. "I'm sorry I ruined your marriage."

I'd told him we decided to separate to give ourselves some space to think about our marriage and reevaluate things, because there was no way I was going to tell him his father didn't want him living under the same roof as his sister. Emotions rose in my throat, but I worked hard to control my voice and keep my face expressionless. "You didn't ruin our marriage. It's not over. It's just different. Things have changed."

"Yeah, because of me." He pulled his hand away. I reached over and took his hand in mine, squeezing tightly.

"Listen, you aren't responsible for anything going on between me and your dad. None of this is your fault. Do you hear me?"

He nodded, but he didn't believe me any more than I believed myself.

*****

I watched as Noah eyed the apartment, nervous about his reaction to the space. He sized up the rooms and meager surroundings—the living room filled with our secondhand couch and the TV balancing on the stand in front of the other wall. It was only a few steps into the kitchen lined with cracked linoleum and cupboards that didn't completely close because they'd been painted so many times. A small folding table with two aluminum chairs functioned as our dining room. I put fresh flowers in a pretty blue vase yesterday hoping it would brighten up the room.

"Not our old house, huh? It's a little rough around the edges, but it grows on you." I did my best to sound happy. "You should've seen what this place looked like before I painted it." I motioned to the empty walls in the living room and dining room. "I waited to put anything up until you got here. There's a really great flea market on Forty-Ninth Street on Saturdays. I thought we could go and pick out pieces together sometime."

"Sure, Mom. Sounds great." He forced a smile, his voice flat. "I'd like that."

There was too much silence between us while we ate dinner. I filled the air with idle conversation, trying to fill up the space. It just like when I visited him in treatment. He was polite, kind, and well-mannered. He smiled when it was appropriate and answered questions when asked, but his eyes were emotionless and there wasn't any life behind his words. He didn't get excited about anything. My lively boy had been replaced with a Stepford Wife.

"My room looks nice. Thanks," he said as I tucked him into bed that night, something he hadn't let me do in years.

Out of habit, I reached to brush the hair out of his face, but it was no longer there, so my hand landed on his cheek, and I rubbed the side of his face instead. "It's over, honey. You can relax now."

I sat on the edge of the bed. I held back the urge to lay next to him and wrap my arms tightly around him like I would've done in the past because my previously affectionate son now stiffened at physical touch. I didn't want to make him uncomfortable, so I reached for his hand and took it in mine.

"I love you no matter what," I said.

I'd been telling him it since he was a baby. I couldn't count the number of times over I'd taken him in my arms and said the same thing. When he was a toddler, one of his favorite games to play while we were driving was for me to call out, "Who loves you?"

"Mommy wuvs me!" he'd yell with glee from the backseat.

"How much?"

He'd raise his arms straight up above his head, straining against his seat belt. "This much!"

"No matter what?"

His echoed "no matter what" came out sounding like *no mamma what,* and he'd always collapse into giggles afterward.

Stressing I loved him no matter what was even more important the older he got because he was such a perfectionist. He didn't fail very often, so he took it hard when he did, especially when it came to swimming. It was obvious from his first mommy and me class that he was gifted in the water. Most kids his age were scared and clung to their parents, but I struggled to keep him from leaping out of my arms. He had no interest in learning how to blow bubbles or rowing his arms like a paddleboat. He wanted to learn how to swim for real, and was skilled in all of the strokes by the time he was five. His swimming academy spotted his talent immediately and took an interest in him early on. He started working with a private coach in first grade and by the next year, he was competing in competitions with kids two years older than him.

He had a hard time whenever he didn't perform like he wanted. When he was young, he cried when he didn't come in first and his tears morphed into anger as a teenager if he didn't come in first place. Lucas and I did our best not to put any pressure on him since he put enough on himself.

"Honey, we love you whether you come in first or last," Lucas would always say.

Our most important goal as parents was for our kids to know we loved them based on who they were rather than any external criteria. We tried to keep our compliments and praise focused on qualities about them rather than their performance. It was easy with Katie, but much more difficult with Noah since he was always so focused on his performance. I admired his drive, and it served him well, but I'd always worried about the amount of pressure he put on himself to be the best.

I worried all the pressure took the fun out of swimming, so I was happy when his coaches asked if he'd coach a team of young swimmers during the summer because it'd help him loosen up and put the fun back in it. The first time they asked him was the summer between eighth and ninth grade. The kids on the team were six and seven-year-old kids, and he jumped at the opportunity because they were the same age he'd been when he started competing. He made time to work with them twice a week and attended their meets despite his busy schedule. He loved working with them, and they loved him just as much. By his second summer of teaching, his classes had a wait list.

The first sign something was wrong with Noah was when he abruptly quit coaching halfway through the summer. He didn't tell me he'd quit, and he told me everything. I only found out because one of his supervisors called to ask me what was going on and if Noah was okay. I'd been shocked. It was so out of character for him to quit anything, especially if it was related to swimming.

"Andy called me today and told me you quit coaching the pee-wee league. What happened?" I asked him at dinner that night.

He shrugged his shoulders, refusing to look at me.

"What? You quit coaching?" Lucas asked. He was as shocked as I'd been.

Noah stared down at his plate of lasagna. "I can't do it anymore. I've got to focus on my own stuff right now."

"But the kids love you," I said. He had an amazing ability to work with them. It could be such a difficult age to hold their attention, but he made their lessons fun.

He shrugged his shoulders again.

"It's the middle of the session. You can't leave them hanging. Don't you think you should at least finish out the summer season?" Lucas asked.

He shook his head.

I looked at Lucas, and we exchanged the "it's his age" look in the same way we did when he was two and throwing a fit because his peanut butter and jelly sandwich was cut in squares when he wanted triangles. Every parent fears the adolescent years, and we were no different.

We'd been waiting for the tumultuousness of adolescence to hit and holding our breath, hoping to be spared, but over the next few weeks, he transformed before our eyes. From out of nowhere, his former bravado was gone and replaced with a teenage slump. He stopped showering regularly, his greasy hair always hanging into his eyes. He no longer cared about his looks and wore the same clothes for days. He usual engaged chatter disappeared and was replaced with one-word answers.

At first, I wrote it off as normal, joking with my friends about how my little boy had disappeared overnight and been replaced with an alien. We all shared our stories about the ways our teenagers were changing, and most of them were similar to mine.

"He never comes out of his room anymore," I complained over coffee after a PTA meeting.

The president, Rochelle, burst out laughing. "Don't worry. When my boys were teenagers, I don't think I saw them for three years."

It was helpful not to feel so alone, but I couldn't erase the gnawing in my gut that something was wrong despite what they said. My fears were magnified when he stopped hanging out with his friends. Our home had always been filled with them. He rarely came home from school alone, and I used to joke about needing another refrigerator to feed them all, but I secretly loved being the house where they all hung out. He stopped bringing anyone home, and no longer spent time anywhere besides his room, the door shut tight behind him.

I kept trying to get him to talk to me, but he refused. He snapped at me when I asked, or rolled his eyes and said everything was fine. I didn't know what to do or how to help him. We'd always been able to talk about anything. I listened when my kids talked. I didn't pretend like I was when I was really thinking about something else. I paid attention to what they told me. Always had. I wanted to be the one they were comfortable talking to about the things happening in their lives and to create an environment where they felt safe coming to me when they were in trouble.

I couldn't accept his denial that there wasn't anything wrong when there so clearly was. I wasn't like other parents, who were too afraid to dig deeper into their child's life and risk upsetting them. Not me. I was convinced he was on drugs and started searching his room regularly but kept coming up empty-handed.

Lucas was just as worried. "I always thought Katie would be the tough teenager," he said. "I've never really worried about him before. It feels so weird."

We doubled our efforts, wracking our brains to come up with new ways to draw him out. Lucas dragged him out of bed on Saturday mornings to go fishing, but he sat like a lump on the side of the river the entire time, often wandering off by himself into the woods. Lucas bought new running shoes and suggested they start training for a marathon together. Lucas hated running, and the idea of him making it twenty-six miles was ridiculous, but he was willing to try anything. Noah refused to go, barely acknowledging his dad's efforts, whereas before he would've teased his father relentlessly about his running skills.

We took turns trying to get him to open up on the weekly date nights we had with each of the kids. Friday was my night with Katie, and Wednesday was Noah's turn. Kid date nights started shortly after Katie was born, during the days when the incessant demands of an infant stole all our attention. We'd wanted Noah to know he was still special and important, so we'd started taking him out by himself. We added Katie to the practice once she was old enough so both of them could have special individual time with each of us.

Wednesdays were my favorite day with Noah. Lots of teenagers would've been embarrassed to be seen hanging out with their mom, but not Noah. He searched for me in the carpool lane on the afternoons when he didn't have practice, and his face slid into a wide smile when he spotted my car. He liked going out on our dates especially because I let him choose the place, but his behavior surrounding Wednesdays and our relationship changed too. More and more, he was refusing to go, making up excuses about homework or having to study for a big test the next day.

"Can we stay home tonight?" he asked after I'd knocked on his door and told him it was time to go on the evening of our last date night.

Disappointment washed over me. He'd gotten out of our date the previous week, and I'd put a lot of thought into this one. I'd chosen his favorite restaurant and decided I wouldn't pressure him to talk at all, hoping he'd do it on his own if I quit pushing so hard.

"Let's go out. I already made reservations at Sawatdee. Besides, you skipped out on me last week, remember?" I stood talking to the wooden door.

He let out a deep sigh. "I really don't feel like going out. What if we popped some popcorn and watched a movie here?"

I didn't want to risk pushing him further away, so I relented. "I'll pop the popcorn, but you've got to meet me in the family room in ten minutes. Deal?"

"Sure," he said without any enthusiasm.

I felt nervous as I made the popcorn. I'd never been unsure about how to approach Noah. I knew him better than I knew myself and could tell his moods and what he was thinking just by looking at his face, but I was losing my ability to read him. It was a normal part of adolescence, but it didn't make it any easier.

We were halfway through our movie when he hit pause and turned to look at me with a look in his eyes I'd never seen before. His eyes filled with tears. "I need to talk to you."

I breathed a sigh of relief that he was finally ready. I grabbed the remote from his hand, flicked the power off, and turned to face him. I sat cross-legged next to him on the couch, ready to listen to whatever he had to tell me. I braced myself for him to tell me he was on drugs.

The tears in his eyes spilled down his cheeks, and he began to sob. I took him in my arms. "It's okay. Whatever it is. We'll work it out. I promise." I started to rub his back.

He pushed me away, detangling himself. "I c-can't. I can't talk about it." He was crying so hard it was difficult to make out his words.

"Honey, you have to talk about it. Keeping things inside destroys you. Things are never as bad as they seem when you're keeping them a secret."

His entire body shook. A torrent of sobs ripped through him, and I didn't say anything while he cried. I tried to hold him again and this time, he let me. He gripped my shirt in the back and buried his head on my shoulder like he'd done when he was a little boy. I held him until his sobs subsided and he pulled away, leaving trails of snot and tears behind. He shook his head, embarrassed at his outburst.

He jumped up and began pacing the living room, back and forth, rubbing his arms up and down with his hands. His eyes were wild, flitting around the room. I was hoping it was only pot he was smoking, but as he grew more agitatcd, I started to worry it was meth, and our problem was much bigger than I'd originally thought.

"Do you promise to love me no matter what?" He looked down at me like a frightened bird.

"Of course, Noah. There's nothing you could say or do that would ever change how I feel about you." I hadn't moved from my spot on the couch. I was determined to follow his lead on this one. Let him get it out in whatever way he needed to.

"I did something terrible." His voice quivered with emotion.

I steeled myself, holding on to the couch with both hands. Had he stolen money to pay for his drugs? Was he wrapped up with some crazy drug dealer? I tried to listen without emotion.

He gulped, hiccupping on the sobs threatening to come up again. "Really bad, Mom. I'm a terrible person." His face twisted with grief. "I'm so scared."

My mouth went dry.

"I can't believe I did it. I don't know what to do. I don't know what's wrong with me. Something's really wrong." His words tripped over each other. "I touched those girls. I did. I touched them."

"What girls? What are you talking about?"

I'd been steeling myself for his confession about trouble with drugs, and it was only a stupid girl making him crazy. I felt a twinge of hurt that he hadn't shared he had a girlfriend, but there had to be a reason he didn't want me to know and it didn't matter now as long as he was talking to me. They must've broken up. First relationships were always brutal. I felt like my world was ending when my high school boyfriend broke up with me.

"Maci and Bella," he said under his breath.

I flipped through the names of girls he hung out with or ones he talked about before, but couldn't remember anyone named Maci or Bella. Maybe they didn't go to his school. He could've met them online. I'd warned him about meeting people online.

"How'd you meet them?" I asked.

"I coach them."

"Did you decide to take on a private client?"

"No, God, Mom, you don't get it." He was raking his hands up and down his arms so hard that I was afraid he'd leave marks. "They're six years old."

Shockwaves wracked my body. Black spots spun in front of my eyes. My dinner came up in my throat. I forced it back down. My hands shook.

"Sit down. Tell me what happened." I didn't recognize the

sound of my voice.

I tried to keep my expression impassive and hide my revulsion toward what he had to say, what he was admitting to. He perched next to me on the couch, shaking his legs back and forth, wringing his hands together on his lap as he spoke.

"I tried so hard not to. I didn't want to, but I couldn't help myself..."

"W-what did you do?" My breath was rapid and shallow. I put my hand on my chest and instructed myself to breathe slowly.

He brought his knees up to his chest and wrapped his arms around them, curling into himself. He rocked back and forth.

"I touched them ... on ... on their privates." His voice was barely a whisper.

"On purpose?" It had to be a mistake. An accident.

He nodded.

I rearranged my face to hide the shock and horror.

"How many times?" My voice wasn't mine. It belonged to someone else.

"A lot. It's why I had to quit, Mom. I had to. I couldn't stop."

"Oh my God, Noah. Oh my God." I brought my hands up to my face and held them there, holding perfectly still. Not moving. My brain couldn't formulate thoughts. He started talking again, but I couldn't hear him. His voice was muffled and far away. I couldn't speak. The word for what he'd done, who he was, bounced around in my brain, but I couldn't say it. The word wouldn't fit in my mouth.

"Mom?" He reached over to touch me.

I flinched. Ice water shot through my veins.

"Did you hurt Katie?"

"No. I'd never hurt her."

He curled up at the end of the couch. He needed me, but I couldn't move. I didn't want to touch him. Didn't want to be in the same room. I bit back the screams in my throat, the ones that wanted to yell at him to get out of my house and give me my son back. I couldn't connect with the confessed child molester in front of me when that morning he'd been the teenager who studied for his social studies test at the kitchen table and quizzed his sister on her spelling words over a bowl of Cheerios.

All the air was sucked out of the room. I stayed rooted to my spot on the couch. Stunned. Paralyzed with fear and disgust. We sat in silence. I had no idea how much time had passed before he announced he was going to bed.

I felt the annihilation of our world and started to weep uncontrollably. It was so far removed from any of the nightmares I'd imagined having to deal with. Like every parent, I'd imagined all kinds of scenarios that could happen to my children—illness, death, accidents, being kidnapped—but in every scenario, I'd pictured them as the victim. None of them included him in the role of the perpetrator. I'd imagined all of it. But this? Never this? This couldn't be my son.

I couldn't stand the thought of facing Lucas or Katie when they got home from their date night. Lucas would take one look at me and know something was wrong. I forced my body to stand and move upstairs. I lay down like I was in a trance and pretended to sleep as I listened for the sounds of them coming home. I didn't move when Lucas got into bed with me.

"It's early. You okay?" he asked.

"I have a horrible headache." I tried to sound sleepy.

I got up once I was sure he was asleep. I paced back and forth down the hallway separating Noah and Katie's rooms, tortured with questions. How did I live with him all these years and never notice something was wrong with him? Nothing amiss. Would it be possible to live with him all those years and not have any idea? How could I not know? I was his mother. Nothing he'd done matched the son I knew and loved.

As I lay next to him on his first night out of Marsh, I wished for the thousandth time I'd handled his confession differently. I failed him during the most critical point in his life, and I wasn't sure I'd ever forgive myself for rejecting him when he needed me the most. I'd give anything to go back in time and reverse my actions. He'd been afraid of me not loving him anymore, and I did exactly what he feared. It didn't matter that I'd been making up for it every day since or that I'd gone into his room in the morning and apologized for the way I'd handled myself and told him how much I still loved him, how I promised we'd get through it, and that I loved him no matter what. It was my fault he disappeared, and I was afraid of never getting him back.

6

The green grass in front of the courthouse was immaculate, but it was only a matter of time before it was covered in dirty white snow. I'd been here at every season, from the red leaves in the fall to the blazing heat in the summer. It never mattered what it looked like outside, though, it was always cold on the inside. I pushed open the heavy wooden doors behind the pillars, bracing myself for what was to come.

I was well versed in the routine. We emptied our pockets into the white plastic trays, and I set my purse in another. We stepped through the security arms one at a time. I was motioned through without a second glance, but Noah wasn't as lucky. He never was. They swabbed him from top to bottom with the security wand while I gathered our things.

Our first stop was the city clerk to check in. She was where you went when you didn't know where to go, and today was new for us—the next step in our journey. We didn't talk as we walked up to her window. She was innocent looking, with blond hair and a round face.

"We're here to register," I said quietly so no one behind us might overhear.

She raised her eyebrows. “Register? For what?”

“As a sex offender.” The word rolled easily off my tongue even though the emotional reaction was always the same.

She pointed to Noah first and then me. “Which one?”

“Me,” Noah said.

“What’s your name?” She shot him a scathing look.

“Noah Coates.”

She typed quickly into the computer and turned up her nose as she read. She tapped a few more buttons and paper shot out of the printer next to her computer. She slid it under the glass with a pen and paper.

“Here.” Disgust flickered through her eyes. Her stare slid from him to me, seething hatred as her eyes landed on me, breathing contempt. I was familiar with the look. It was the one everyone gave me when they found out who he was.

Noah signed himself in and slid the paperwork back underneath the glass along with the pen. She didn’t take her eyes off me as he handed her his information. She used her folder to push the pen he used to the top of her desk as if it was contaminated. I reminded myself of what Dr. Park always said in family groups, “We are not our loved ones’ crimes,” hoping this time it would make a difference, but it never does. Noah wasn’t just guilty—we all were. And once you were dirty, you couldn’t get clean again. You were like a chewed piece of gum.

“Where do we go?” I asked, keeping my head held high and my shoulders back.

She pointed to the right. “Down the hallway, take your first left, and then your second right.”

We walked down the hallway with faces of important-looking people housed in wooden frames lining the walls. I recognized two of them as Jefferson and Washington. Our footsteps echoed as we walked. It was always so quiet. We found the office we were looking for and a short man with broad shoulders and an angular jaw greeted us after we opened the door.

He stood from behind his desk and stuck his hand out to me. "I'm Sheriff Anderson." He didn't shake Noah's hand. Nobody does. "Have a seat." He pointed to the chairs in front of his wooden desk, cluttered with papers and folders. I fought the urge to tidy them up as we took our seats.

"What's your plan?" he asked.

He was referring to the safety plan—the one the last three weeks of treatment were spent creating. I made three copies, one for me, one for Lucas—although I didn't think he ever read it—and one for the sheriff. I pulled it out of my purse and handed it to him. His forehead crinkled as he read through the document. The clock on the wall ticked. I could hear Noah breathing next to me.

"How are you going to make sure he's not offending again?" he asked, finally looking up from the paper.

"He's gotten help and so have I. I'll be able to recognize his symptoms because we've talked about them, and I know what to look for," I said with a calm I didn't feel. Noah's expression was impassive and didn't change as the conversation moved around him.

Sheriff Anderson dug through the piles of paperwork on his desk, finding what he was looking for and handing it to me. "Here's the conditions of his probation. Give it a read through."

The conditions of his probation were what I'd expected. No

unsupervised contact with young children, no contact with his victims, no use of pornographic materials, and no Internet. He would submit to monthly drug testing even though he'd never shown any signs of drug use. He wasn't allowed to drink alcohol or be where it was served. He couldn't leave the state of Illinois without permission. He had to follow his safety plan. And lastly, what we were there for today—he had to register as a sex offender.

I had tried to fight his registration as a sex offender, but it was useless because of the Adam Walsh Act. I'd never heard of the act until Noah's conviction. It was formed in response to the kidnapping and brutal murder of Adam Walsh. Adam's father hosted *America's Most Wanted* after his son was kidnapped and fought for stricter registration laws after he was found murdered years later by a known sex offender.

Twenty-seven states had enacted registration laws. There were three tiers of registration based on the type of offense and the person's likelihood to reoffend. Tier Three was the worst and required lifetime supervision and checking in with the state every ninety days. Noah was a Tier One offender. He'd be listed on the national registry for ten years and had to verify his identity and location once a year with the local sheriff's department.

It didn't matter that I understood why the register was there. I still hated it. Every situation was unique and had to be judged by its own merit. You couldn't blindly lump Noah into categories and classifications. Every school, college, and job for the next ten years would know he was a sex offender.

He'd done his time, gone to treatment, and followed through on everything they'd asked him to do, but he was still being punished. What was the point of treatment if he wasn't going to have the opportunity to do anything they taught him there? The goal on all Marsh's pamphlets and materials touted success in helping the convicted teen live a prosocial life without further legal involvement. The graduation plan stressed the importance of starting over in the community and family reunification. How was he supposed to do any of it when he wore a scarlet letter branded on his forehead?

"Do you understand what this means?" It was the first time he'd spoken to Noah.

"I get it." Noah stared at his shoes without looking up.

Sheriff Anderson slid the documents across his desk and handed us pens. Noah didn't bother to read any of it before signing on the line. I skimmed through it briefly, but it wasn't anything I hadn't read before. I added my signature to the required line and provided the sheriff with all our contact information. Just like that, it was over, and Noah's future was sealed.

*****

Katie ran at Noah and threw herself into his arms as soon as we walked through the door of their house. He scooped her up and swung her around wildly as she giggled.

"That's enough," Lucas said from his spot at the kitchen table.

I shot him a look.

Noah stopped and plopped her onto the floor, ruffling the hair on top of her hand. She clung to his arm, wrapping herself around him.

"I'm so glad you're home. Come on, I want to show you the picture I made for you." She grabbed his hand and skipped into the living room.

Lucas followed behind and hovered over them with his chest puffed out and arms crossed as they knelt by the coffee table.

"See, look, it's us." She pointed to a rainbow with two sets of swings hanging from it. One held a blond girl, and the other a larger, brown-haired boy. They were smiling and holding hands as they swung.

"What's that?" Noah asked, pointing to a small black dog in the picture.

"That's the dog we're going to get."

I laughed. She'd been begging for a dog since she learned how to talk.

"Really? Since when were you able to talk Dad into getting a dog?" Noah asked.

Lucas had a strict no-pet policy because of his allergies. The only pets the kids were allowed to have were goldfish, but somehow we managed to kill more than we ever kept. Eventually, we gave up trying.

"I've been reconsidering," Lucas said.

"Are you serious?" Noah asked.

Lucas looked uncomfortable whenever Noah spoke to him, and tonight was no different. I wanted to shake him. Why couldn't he just try a little bit?

"Maybe." He shrugged.

"But, Daddy, you said it'd help me not miss Noah so much."

Lucas turned bright red and worked his jaw. Noah's momentary light that Katie sparked was extinguished. I stepped into the center of the living room.

"How about we eat some pizza?" I asked, trying to shift the

mood.

We filed into the kitchen in silence. Katie looked back and forth between Lucas and me, trying her best to read what was going on. She sat in the chair next to Noah.

"I'm sitting here from now on," she said.

She used to sit in the chair across from him. I wanted to cry at how hard she was trying to prove her solidarity. Lucas took his seat at the head of the table, and I brought in the pizza we ordered earlier. I passed around the paper plates. My appetite was gone, but I forced myself to take two pieces. Lucas did the same. Katie dug into hers. The rest of ours sat untouched.

I pulled my phone out of my pocket and pulled up Lucas's number.

For God's sake, you can at least try. He's your son.

I hit send. He pulled his phone out of his pocket. He didn't bother to look at me as he texted a response, setting it next to him on the table when he was finished. I waited a few minutes before looking at my phone because I didn't want Noah to figure out we were texting each other.

I'm doing my best.

I'd seen him do his best, and this didn't come close. He wasn't doing anything. It'd been eighteen months since Noah's confession. He had a year and a half to get used to things. To adjust. Find a new normal, but he hadn't changed since the night he found out.

Noah didn't want to tell Lucas what he'd done, and begged me to do it for him, but I refused. I told him I'd help him, but he had to be a part of it. I waited until Katie had gone to bed and I was sure she was asleep before I went up to Noah's room to let him know it was time. We headed into the living room together. Lucas was sitting in the recliner thumbing through the stack of reports he'd brought home from work. I sat on the couch and motioned for Noah to take a seat next to me. He sat next to me, his body stiff and rigid.

"Noah has something to share with you." I chose my words carefully. "I want to warn you that this is going to be hard to hear. I want you to take a deep breath and prepare yourself."

His eyes filled with fear. "What's going on? Noah? What's wrong?"

Noah shook his head.

"Noah?" he asked again.

Noah kept shaking his head.

"Last night Noah and I talked about what's been going on with him. He told me about a problem he's having." I couldn't believe I was going to have to say it out loud. I was praying he'd handle it better than I did. "We're a family and no matter what, we'll get through this." I turned to look at Noah, hoping he believed me. "Remember that he's our son. We love him—"

Lucas cut me off. "What's going on?"

"I—"

"Adrianne, what is going on?"

"Noah molested two of the girls on the pee-wee league." My voice came out almost a whisper. It was the first time I'd said it.

The color drained from Lucas's face. His eyes bulged. He clamped his hand over his mouth, jumped up from his spot, and sprinted to the bathroom in the hallway. I heard the sound of his vomit splattering on the tiled floor. My stomach turned over at the sounds of him retching violently. The putrid smell of acidic vomit filled the room.

He stepped out of the bathroom looking like a madman. Puke crusted the front of his shirt. His eyes were still wide and unblinking, but now they were bright red from popped blood vessels. His entire body shook.

"Lucas, sit down. Just sit back down," I said softly.

He didn't move or speak, just looked right through me like he wasn't seeing me. I stood, taking cautious steps toward him. He turned and bolted for the kitchen. I followed him just as the door slammed shut behind him. Noah whimpered in the living room. I rushed back to him. I took him in my arms and rocked him.

"He's just in shock. It's really hard to hear. We've got to give him a minute to get himself together." I kept rocking him back and forth like I'd done when he was a baby. His rigid body slowly went limp in my arms. "I'm so sorry for how I handled things last night. I wish—"

He lifted his head. "Mom, don't. I get it. I totally understand." He lay back against me.

Lucas wasn't gone long before he walked through the living room. He didn't even glance in our direction before he headed upstairs. Soon, we heard banging above us.

"Stay here," I instructed Noah.

I found Lucas in the hallway outside of Katie's room with his toolbox spread open beside him. He was tugging and jerking at her doorknob, trying to pull it out of the circular hole. Sweat poured from his forehead.

"What are you doing?" I asked.

He didn't speak, just pointed to the packaging laying at his feet—a new doorknob. I picked it up. It had a lock. None of our kids' bedrooms had locks because we didn't want to take the chance of them accidentally getting locked inside.

"Mommy?" Katie called out.

"Go back to sleep, sweetie. Daddy's fixing your door."

I went slack against the wall next to him. I sat while he worked. It didn't take him long to install the new doorknob.

"You have to go down there and talk to him," I said.

"I'm not talking to him." He moved past me in the hallway and into the bathroom to brush his teeth.

He slept on the floor of Katie's bedroom that night on the same air mattress I used now. He slept there until Noah went to treatment. He'd never talked to him. Not that night or the next. He quit speaking to him except when Katie was around. He left whenever he came into the room. He spoke around him, but never to him. He looked over him instead of at him. Even during all the meetings with the lawyer and trial, he sat in silence, unmoved.

I understood his shock and the horror. What Noah did was abhorrent, but he was our son. No matter what he'd done, he was still our son. I couldn't sever my love for him any more than I could cut off my arm.

I'd given up trying to talk to Lucas about Noah. It only increased his frustration with me. We moved around the topic of him like skilled dancers performing a beautiful ballet. But we weren't going to be able to ignore it any longer. He was out. He was here, sitting at our kitchen table eating pizza.

HIM(THEN)

My shirt is plastered against me with sweat. It's my turn now, and I know how this goes. I hate this part of therapy. I keep telling myself it will be different—that this time it's going to work, and I'm not going to react.

The electrodes are strapped to my head. I think that's why they shave our heads, because how would we ever get the sticky glue off if they didn't? I don't even bother trying to get all of it off anymore. Pieces of it are permanently stuck to my pillows.

They never talk about this part with our parents. Does Mom know what they do to me? What these sessions consist of? She can't because she'd never allow it if she did. But I can't tell her. It's another secret I have to keep. There's so many secrets about this place and I can't tell any of them because I don't want to cause trouble or have any marks against me. Not with staff or the other kids. So far I have a flawless record, and I plan on keeping it that way. I'll do what they say. Everything. All of it. Not just because I want to get out, but because I want to get better. More than anything.

It's why this is so hard. Every time we have one of these sessions I hope I won't react. That their pictures will mean nothing, and I'll come through the session without any shocks. But I never do. It's only a matter of time before my body responds. It rarely happens when I look at the first few pictures, but after a while it does. I can't help myself. I have no control over it, and I hate myself for it.

The shocks are supposed to train my brain. Help me think and respond differently. They keep promising me that it will work if I do it long enough. Eventually my brain will look at a picture of a young girl and remember the shock instead of the arousal.

I have to believe them. They're doctors, so they've got to know what they're doing, and they have to fix me. It's what they're trained to do. I can't stay this way. I just can't. Most of the other boys don't even care, but I do. All I want is to get better and be normal.

I never knew there was something wrong with me. There weren't any clues. One day it just happened. It was like a switch went on and once it'd been turned on, I couldn't turn it off no matter how hard I tried. And I really did try. I never wanted to hurt anyone. But I did, and now it's my job to make sure I never do it again.

The door opens and the nurse walks in carrying the machine with all the weird wires coming out of it. My doctor is next to her.

"Are you ready?" the nurse asks, smiling at me.

I nod, too nervous to speak. Maybe today will be the day.

7

I wasn't sure who was more nervous for his first day at school. Him or me. I barely slept the night before and by the sounds of Noah's tossing and turning, he hadn't either.

"What do you want me to fix you?" I asked in the morning.

"Just coffee."

I whipped around. "Coffee? When did you start drinking coffee?"

"At Marsh."

"You—" I shut my mouth. I was going to say he was too young to drink coffee, but it seemed childish now after everything he'd been through. I filled him a cup.

"Do you take cream or sugar?"

"Just black."

"Whoa. You're hardcore." I handed him his mug and took a seat at the table. He clasped his hands around it like a pro, sipping it slowly. "I can't believe you're a senior."

"Never thought my senior year would go down like this, huh?" Somehow his situation worked its way into all of our conversations.

I nodded. “Does it feel weird to wear regular clothes?”

He’d never gone to a public school before, not even in preschool. He didn’t know what it was like to pick out an outfit for school since he’d only worn uniforms.

“It’s kind of strange.” He looked down at his white t-shirt and jeans. His jeans were a little too short, but they’d suffice for the next few days until I could take him shopping and let him pick out his own clothes.

“Are you nervous?”

He shrugged.

“I’m sorry about how your dad acted last night.”

We hadn’t talked about it yet. He was sullen and quiet on the drive home. His silence was a welcome relief because I didn’t know what to say about Lucas and refused to justify his behavior. I couldn’t imagine what it was like for Noah. He and his dad used to be so close.

He stared into his coffee mug.

“I want you to know I don’t agree with or support how he treats you,” I said.

Lucas and I decided early on always to maintain a united front in front of our kids. It didn’t matter if we agreed with the other person or not, we would support them in front of the kids. It wasn’t like we’d never disagreed before. We disagreed on a lot of things. Lucas claimed I was too easy on them, and I thought he was too hard. We argued about how much money we spent all the time. Lucas wanted to keep a tighter rein on our finances, but I never agreed. However, our kids had no idea about our differences. We waged our parenting wars behind closed doors.

This was the first time I hadn’t sided with Lucas in front of the kids. I was betraying our agreement, but I couldn't support the way he treated Noah. He needed us more now than he ever had. I wasn't okay Lucas treating him with indifference. I'd seen him treat strangers in our home better than he treated Noah last night. He stood by Katie's side the entire time like he was her bodyguard and at any moment, Noah would attack her. When she clung to him during their good-bye hug, Lucas pulled her away long before she was ready. I was going to have a talk with Katie the next time we were alone just like I was doing with Noah. I didn't care about our agreement anymore.

"I can't imagine how he must make you feel," I said. His head was down, but I could see his lip quivering.

"I miss my dad," he said, swallowing the lump of emotions in his throat.

I knew what it was like to lose your dad. Mine died five years ago, and there was still a hollowness in my heart from his absence. "I know you do. I miss him too."

"Do you think he'll ever forgive me?" He lifted his head. His eyes were filled with so much sadness, I felt it. Nothing cut deeper than seeing one of my children in pain.

"I hope so. I think maybe once he gets used to seeing you again, it might make it easier for him. Hopefully..."

"I don't know how to talk to him."

I got up and knelt beside him at eye level. "It's not your job to figure out how to get him to talk to you. He's your dad. It's his job to figure out how to make things right. I want you to understand that. It's not your fault."

"But it is. I—"

I pushed my finger against his lips. "Shh, don't say it. Noah, you did something awful. You know that, I know that, and your dad knows it too. But, you took responsibility. You've made things right, and eventually your dad is going to have to accept that. There isn't any going backward. What's done is done. None of us can change it. We've got to figure out a way to move forward. Put it behind us. Do you understand?"

He nodded. Tears spilled down his cheeks.

"We'll get through this." I hoped if I said it enough times it would become a reality. "Do you want me to walk to school with you?"

He wiped his nose and picked up his backpack, filled with his lunch and new notebooks. "Nah, I'm okay."

I stood and hugged him, pulling him close. The smell of soap wafted into my nose. I didn't want to let him go. My mama bear instincts kicked in, and I had a fierce desire to protect him from the day, to walk him through it like I walked him through his first day of preschool and kindergarten, but I couldn't. I had to let him go.

"Have a good day," I said.

The vastness of the day stretched out in front of me. I sat down to work on my transcripts, but couldn't concentrate. I kept rewinding the player again and again. After a while, I gave up trying to get any work done. I stared at the clock as the minutes inched by, holding my breath, and waiting for the phone to buzz and tell me something terrible had happened to him. My stomach turned in on itself.

I missed the days when I had friends to call who'd help me feel better. It still hurt that the women I thought were my friends weren't who I thought they were. Once I had children, I naturally developed relationships with other mothers because it made my life easier. All of my friends were mothers with kids around the same ages as mine, and they all shunned me as soon as Noah's story got out. No one said good-bye. They were there one day and gone the next. It was that quick.

I occasionally talked to my childhood best friend, Tracey. She used to ask how I was doing since it was her obligation as my best friend, but she didn't really want to know the answer. In the beginning, I unloaded all the pain and questions I kept locked inside during the day as soon as she picked up the phone. I rambled until I exhausted myself and then there was silence—the horrible silence—until one of us started talking about something completely unrelated, which only made it more awkward. I didn't blame her for not knowing what to say to me. Eventually, I stopped sharing how I felt to save us both from the embarrassment. Now I dodged the questions about myself and volleyed the conversation back at her life, but even that was uncomfortable because I could hear the guilt and hesitation in her voice as she shared the good things happening in her life. The length between our conversations stretched further and further apart.

My mom only lived thirty minutes away and was a huge help with Katie, but she was a strong Catholic woman who didn't believe in talking about problems. Never had. While Noah was in treatment, she always asked how he was doing and when he was coming home, but in a singsong voice like he was away at summer camp.

In the past few years, Lucas spent more time with her than I did. He'd been taking care of her since my father died. My parents were together for thirty-eight years, and she had relied on my dad for everything. He'd always taken care of her, and she was lost without him. I expected it to get easier for her over time, but it didn't. It'd been five years since he died, but my mother struggled to make it through each day. I used to think it was sweet that Lucas was there for her like he was—shoveling her snow in the winter, mowing her lawn in the summer, fixing things around the house, managing her finances—but it all changed when our family needed him, and he couldn't be there for us in the same way. How could he care for her like he did and ignore his own son?

Lucas could do no wrong in her eyes. He was like the son she never had, and he cherished their maternal relationship since his parents were gone. Lucas's parents passed away shortly after we got married, and taking care of my mother helped fill the void they left. I'd pushed her to try to approach him about how he responded to Noah, but she refused.

"Oh heavens, Adrianne. Leave the poor boy alone. He has so much on his plate. He'll come around," she said each time I tried.

But he wasn't coming around. I hoped seeing Noah after so much time had passed would kickstart his deadened parental instincts, because how could he watch Noah interact with Katie last night and not have his heart soften at least a little? What was I going to do if things stayed this way? Even if I lived separately with Noah until he went to college, he was still going to be part of our lives. He'd be going away to college, not dying.

Lucas's actions would be easier to understand if he was a man naturally cut off from his emotions, but he wasn't, despite working with numbers and math formulas all day. He'd always been openly affectionate, free with his smiles, and easily moved to tears by things the kids did like when Katie created her first comic book, or Noah read a sentence all by himself without any help. He was also fiercely protective over them. When Katie was in preschool, there was a toddler who bit the other kids and Lucas organized a group of parents to get the child removed from school even though the kids were only three years old. In third grade, Noah's teacher questioned whether he'd read the number of books he'd read in order to win a reading competition. Lucas was furious she'd doubted his integrity and ability. He set up a meeting with her and sent the assistant principal a letter detailing his concerns. His efforts resulted in an apology to Noah from his teacher along with a free pizza from Pizza Hut for winning the reading competition.

I was unbelievably lonely but rarely allowed myself to admit it. There were times when the debilitating aloneness threatened to swallow me like a black hole and today was one of those days, but I'd gotten used to breaking up my days into manageable moments to get through them. It was the only way I'd survived the last two years. When I was paralyzed with fear and assaulted with my emotions, I stopped and asked myself, what do I need to do right now? And then I did it.

It got me through the early days when I was afraid of falling apart and not being put back together again. It was like a death occurred in our family, but unlike most losses, there was nobody to help and support us through it. There weren't any calls or visits. No meals dropped off on our porch. There wasn't a service or a ceremony. No kind words or condolences. Usually, when you were in a state of grief, people stepped gingerly around you. They were careful not to break you any more than you'd already been broken. They were gentle and kind, speaking in quiet tones as if you might crumble if they spoke too loudly. Not so with us. There was no kindness. No sympathy. Nobody acknowledged our world had been destroyed. I was completely alone in my grief and loss.

Time had dragged. Nobody told me time slowed down with tragedy and how each minute became excruciating when it was painful to merely exist. Just when I was gaining my footing, something would remind me of it and send me into an emotional tailspin. Most of the time it was the little things, like a college admission packet in the mail, an email about ordering hot lunches for the next month, or lyrics to a song he liked. The grief would pummel me, and I had no choice except to succumb to it until it passed.

I felt the talons of it reaching out to me now and pushed it aside like it was a real entity. I grabbed my phone and tapped out Lucas's number. He answered on the third ring.

"I was waiting for you to call," he said.

"Why didn't you call, then?"

"I didn't want to disrupt your morning. I thought maybe you had a lot of work to do."

He knew me better than that. Even if I had a stack of reports piling up, I wouldn't be able to concentrate. Not when something important was going on with one of my kids.

"What'd you think of last night?" I didn't bother with small talk. I didn't have it in me today.

Dead air, then finally, "He looked weird."

"I know, right? It's so strange to see him with short hair."

"I don't know. It's not just the hair. He doesn't really look like himself anymore. He's so tall."

Of course he looked different. He hadn't seen him in over a

year, but I didn't want to fight so I kept my comments to myself. More than anything, I just wanted to talk about our kids like we used to.

"I think it's safe to say he made it through the awkward phase okay," I said.

We always joked about how distorted boys looked when they went through puberty—nothing right-sized or in proportion as they morphed from boys to men.

He laughed, but it was strained. "Yeah, I guess so."

"Katie was so happy, huh? Are you really going to get a dog?"

He laughed. This time, it sounded real. "I made the mistake of suggesting it one night when she was really bummed. You know how she is. She latched onto it and hasn't let go since."

"Do you want to do dinner again tonight?"

"I don't think we can."

I knew Katie's schedule and there wasn't anything going on, but I didn't push.

"Okay. Maybe tomorrow," I said.

"Maybe..." He cleared his throat. "Listen, I've got to go. I've got a meeting in a few minutes."

"Okay. Love you."

"Bye."

He didn't say he loved me too. I couldn't remember the last time he had.

HIM(THEN)

Mark tried to kill himself yesterday. He was only thirteen, one of the youngest boys here. The others picked on him constantly. Joe started it. He always does. He targeted Mark as soon as he found out Mark had molested his younger sister. Joe's reasoning about right and wrong defies all logic. Even though he's here for raping a ten-year-old boy while he was in foster care and threatening to kill him, he thinks people that mess with their female relatives are sick and disgusting. Like they're the ones with a problem and should be punished. There's a strange hierarchy of crimes here, and I still don't understand it. I'm not sure I want to.

I wish there was a way to keep our crimes a secret but we can't. Telling the group what we did is part of our treatment process. Staff calls it Disclosure and says it's to teach us accountability. You can't get past level one until you complete Disclosure, which means admitting to your core treatment group the crimes you committed, the names of your victims, and what you did to them. Some of the boys stay on level one for months because they won't do it or they only tell half-truths. I don't know why they refuse or try to hide anything. It's not like our counselors don't already know our rap sheets. We bring them with us when we come.

Mark was quick to disclose his crime, and I watched Joe's eyes fill with fury as Mark described molesting his youngest sister. Joe has five sisters, and he says you don't mess with blood, so Mark never stood a chance. I wanted to warn him because he seemed so innocent, but I didn't dare. I'm still one of the lucky ones who has never been on the receiving end of Joe's wrath.

Joe made his life miserable. He raped him in the shower the way he does to the young ones, but his torture didn't stop there. He took every opportunity he could to hurt him. He spat in his lunch tray as if the food wasn't disgusting enough as it was and during school, he'd walk by and smear boogers on his desk while he worked. On the yard, he hit him with balls over and over again, laughing about how he'd overthrown the basket, but we all knew he did it on purpose. Mark didn't dare tell. We all know better than to snitch. It didn't take long for Mark to crumble.

They found him in his room with a belt around his neck. He'd tied it to his doorknob and shut the door. He was unconscious by the time staff arrived, and I've never seen them move so fast. The paramedics stuck a weird tube down his throat while we all huddled in the doorway to watch. The counselors called an emergency meeting this afternoon and told us he's going to make it, but he won't be coming back here after he gets out of the hospital. He's going to be transferred to a psychiatric unit instead.

It's all anyone talked about today. Everyone keeps saying he was a wimp and calling him crazy, laughing about how weak he was. I kept my mouth shut like I always do, but they're wrong. He isn't a wimp. He's brave. I wish I wasn't so afraid to take my own life, but I'm terrified of what comes after. I don't know what scares me more—some kind of afterlife or nothing at all. I think about what it would be like to do it all the time. It's been that way ever since I hurt those girls. Sometimes the only way I can fall asleep at night is to pretend I'm dead.

He also wasn't crazy. It's not insane to want to die when you don't have anything to live for and he didn't. Why should be bother staying alive? Why am I?

I hate days like this when the darkness overtakes me. It's so heavy. I try to think about something happy, but all my memories are tainted now. Nothing is pure. Everything is as dirty as I am.

8

Noah and I fell into a routine with each day blending into the next. It was easier than I expected. He came home from school sullen and depressed while I made dinner and nagged him to do his homework, something I'd never had to do before. I tried to get him to talk while we ate, but each attempt only pushed him further into silence. He was relieved when dinner was over, and we settled on the couch to watch TV where our conversations centered on whatever show we were currently binge-watching on Netflix.

He was struggling at school even though he wouldn't talk about it. He hadn't made any friends. High school never changed despite all the changes in the world around it. It was heaven for those who were in and hell for those who weren't. Noah never had to contend with being on the outside. He'd been the center of things with everyone else orbiting around him. He didn't have the skills for infiltrating groups and merging into social circles when he'd always been the one who created them. He was utterly alone at a time when friends were the most important thing in your life. Not being allowed on the Internet only made his situation worse and increased his sense of isolation.

I toyed with the idea of contacting his former best friend, Kyle. He was the closest thing he had to a sibling like before Katie came along. Kyle spent so much time at our house he had his own toothbrush in the bathroom. They developed a secret language that they used until fifth grade. The two of them rarely fought. When they did, they tangled like cats until they were pulled apart, but it was over quickly, and they were back to doing whatever they'd been doing before. They finished each other's sentences, laughed at the same jokes, and played the same sports. They started running cross country together in seventh grade and during every race they ran side by side for the first three miles pacing each other. They only broke stride in the last fifty meters before the finish line, where they sprinted to the end.

Kyle's mom, Janice, and I took turns lugging them to and from practice. She was someone I wouldn't have been friends with if our children weren't friends. I'd always been like Katie, quiet and reserved, so Janice's loud and outspoken personality wasn't one I normally bonded with. She dressed as wildly as she talked, but we grew close over the years since we spent so much time together.

Those relationships were gone. Janice was one of the leaders who organized the committee to flyer our neighborhood. She forbade Kyle to have any contact with Noah and didn't allow them to say good-bye to each other. Noah tried to call him once shortly after it happened, and she told him never to call their house again or speak to Kyle if he saw him anywhere. He was devastated.

Had Noah's time away changed things? What would happen if I called Kyle and tested the waters? Maybe Janice would be more relaxed since he'd completed his treatment, but my hopes fell when I remembered the locker room incident. Kyle wasn't part of beating Noah, but he watched and did nothing. No amount of time would change that.

Noah was the happiest when Katie was around. I was too. She was the bright spot in our week. We looked forward to her visits at the apartment. It'd been weeks since we'd gone to Lucas's house. His house was too depressing and his constant hovering overshadowed everything. It was easier to have her here where he wouldn't bother us. He left us alone at the apartment and hadn't stepped foot in the door since he helped me move in. He wouldn't even come inside when he dropped her off.

I picked her up from school on Mondays, Wednesdays, and Fridays. She squealed with delight each time she got in the car and saw Noah. They helped me prepare dinner when we got home, and her chatter was a welcome break from trying to fill the empty silence that surrounded Noah and me while we ate. She prattled about her day, and the stories she was working on. She wanted to be a graphic novelist when she grew up, and she created elaborate fantasies and fairy tales. She was a great storyteller, and we loved listening to her describe the characters. Noah relaxed in her presence. It was the only time the rigidity left his body. His words flowed easily and naturally with her. I loved the effect she had on him.

After we ate, we cleaned the dishes and set the table with the cards for Forbidden Island. It was a new game Katie discovered while playing at her friend's house and advanced enough that we didn't feel like we were playing a children's game. The goal was to capture all the treasures on the island before the island sank into the flood waters and all was lost. Unlike most games, we worked as a team rather than competing against each another. We giggled and laughed as we moved our pieces across the board.

Hope rose inside me on the nights she visited. They lit up in each other's presence like they'd always done, and the Noah I remembered came out as he joked with her. He had a kind-hearted way of teasing her that always made her feel special and like she was the most important person in the room. It filled my heart with warmth to watch them. I wished Lucas could see it. It was the one thing that kept it from being perfect.

"Mommy, can I please stay overnight with you guys? Please?" she begged as I got her things ready for her to go home the following Friday.

"I'm sorry. You can't." It was so hard taking her back to Lucas. I hated it and wanted her to stay as much as she did.

"Please? It's the weekend. I don't have school tomorrow." She stuck her lip out in an exaggerated pout, her brow furrowed with anger.

I shook my head.

"I want to stay." She wasn't one to argue, so her persistence was surprising. "He's not going to hurt me." She put her hands on her hips.

I patted her on the top of her silky blond hair. "I know it's hard to understand, but it's what's best for you."

She jerked away from my touch. "No, it's not. You both are so worried about him hurting me. He's not going to hurt me. He loves me."

I cringed. "Katie, please stop. I don't want to get into this with you. There's a lot about the situation that you don't understand."

She vehemently shook her head. "Yes, I do. You think I don't know what's going on?" She stared at me, daring me to speak. I turned away, putting the rest of the things that she'd need for tomorrow in her backpack. "He hurt those little girls. He touched them on their private parts. I don't care if he touches me on my private parts."

I froze. Still as a statue. We'd never told her he touched the girls on their private parts.

"I know what he did, and I don't care. I'm not afraid of him." She jutted her chin out.

I turned around robotically, staring at her pint-sized body in front of me, her hands still on her hips, her chin jutted out in defiance. I knelt in front of her.

"I'm not afraid of Noah either," I said.

"Then, why can't everything be okay? He made a mistake, but he said he's sorry. Can't everyone just forgive him?" Tears welled in her eyes.

Noah's voice broke in as he came down the hallway. "It's not that easy, Peanut. But you are the sweetest kid on the planet."

She ran to him, throwing her arms around his waist and hugging him tightly. "I love you, Noah. I don't care what you did. I forgive you. You're still my big brother."

He hugged her back, tears streaming unashamed down his face. It broke my heart. It'd been months since I'd seen him cry. He stopped crying while he was at Marsh.

"Yes, I am. I'm still your big brother, and I'd never do anything to hurt you," he said.

Katie whipped around to face me. "See? I told you. Why can't you believe him?"

I wanted to. More than anything.

"Can I call Daddy and ask him? Please can I, Mommy?" She clung to Noah. He shrugged and gave me a sheepish grin.

"Let me call your dad and see if you can stay overnight just this once," I said.

She squealed. "Really? Call him, Mommy. Call him now!"

I grabbed my phone and walked toward my bedroom to talk in private. He wasn't going to say yes without a fight, and I didn't want the kids to hear it. I stopped midstride. Fear gripped me. They were alone in the living room together. My stomach rose in my throat. Did I really trust him? Did I mean what I said about him not hurting her? That she was safe? Was I sure? My brain spun. Would I leave her alone with anyone else who was a confessed child molester? My heart sunk as I rushed back into the living room.

Lucas answered on the second ring.

"Is everything okay?" he asked, instantly concerned since we rarely spoke on the phone anymore. The majority of our conversations were through text messages.

"It's fine. Everything's fine." I tried to sound cheery and light. "Katie would like to spend the night with us tonight, so I was calling to check in with you about it."

She looked up at me from the couch with eager eyes.

"Absolutely not. We've talked about this." His voice was angry.

I plastered a smile on my face and nodded at Katie. "Yes, I understand. Sure. She's so excited. She's going to sleep in my bed with me. Except I'm sure I won't get any sleep with her. You know what a light sleeper I am."

I hoped he could read between words: *She will be with me. I will not let her out of my sight.*

"No. I said no. I'm not changing my mind."

"Okay. I'm glad you understand how much this means to her—"

"Adrianne, don't you dare do this."

"All right, great. I'll have her back after breakfast. We'll see you tomorrow."

I hit end before he had a chance to say anything else. My heart raced. Katie jumped up and down, squealing and clapping.

"I get to stay!"

Noah high-fived her. "So, what do you want to do?"

*****

I didn't sleep at all that night, but it was worth it. It'd been so long since both my children were under the same roof and even longer since they went to sleep with smiles on their faces. The three of us had cuddled on the couch and watched a movie together just like we used to. Afterward, Noah told her stories as she fought sleep for as long as she could until she couldn't keep her eyes open any longer. It was a night like I'd dreamed about so many times while he was gone, even if Lucas was going to be furious with me in the morning. If he was anyone else, he probably would've stormed over to the apartment and dragged Katie out, but he was the only person who hated confrontation more than me.

"Thanks, Mom," Noah whispered as he tucked the blanket underneath her chin. She looked so small curled up in my bed.

"For what?" I asked.

He smiled. "There's no way Dad said it was okay for her to stay here tonight."

"He did. He ju—"

He threw his arm around my shoulders. "You're a terrible liar. Always have been."

I leaned into him, resting my head against his chest. He stroked my hair in the same way I'd done to him so many times in the past. "You're the best. You really are." He kissed my cheek. "I really appreciate what you did. Good night, Mom."

I checked my phone. I hadn't looked at it since I hung up on Lucas. I wanted to enjoy our time together and not be bothered with battling him. To my surprise, he hadn't called or sent me any texts. I quickly tapped one out to him.

Things went really good tonight. Noah is in his room and Katie is asleep next to me.

I waited for a few minutes, but there was nothing. I checked it all night, but never got a response. I tried to pretend like I was staying awake because of excitement, but I grew really tired as the night went on and couldn't deny there was another reason I wouldn't let myself sleep. There was no mistaking what happened to me when I left them alone in the living room. I could no longer say with one hundred percent certainty that Noah wouldn't hurt Katie. I still didn't think he would, but my gut screamed at me in the hallway not to leave them alone. I'd never forgive myself if I left her alone with him and something happened.

It was a crushing blow on top of a wonderful night to have my denial peeled away, but it gave me a measure of understanding for what it must be like for Lucas. I'd been so sure he would never hurt Katie that I hadn't been able to imagine his reality. Until tonight. I'd never experienced that fear before, but Lucas always had. I didn't understand how he could treat Noah like he did, but for the first time, I understood his fear.

I planned on telling him what I'd realized when I dropped Katie off in the morning, but he didn't give me a chance. He ran into the driveway before I turned the car off. Katie bounced out.

"Katie, go inside. I need to talk to your mom." His voice was forced.

She gave me a quick hug and skipped off into the house. He waited until she was inside before speaking again.

"Don't you ever do that or put me in that position again," he hissed through gritted teeth.

"Lucas, it was okay. Everything was fine. The kids—"

He cut me off. "I don't want to hear about it. Any of it. I've been generous. I've gone against my better judgment and allowed her to visit him because it would crush her not to, but she is never to be with him unsupervised. Ever. And—"

This time, I interrupted him. "But she wasn't. I never let them be alone. I didn't even sleep last night. Just to make sure."

"I talked to a lawyer last night. If you ever pull a stunt like that again, there will be consequences." The veins pulsed in his forehead. I'd never seen him mad so mad.

It felt like he took a baseball bat and slammed it in my gut. "You talked to a lawyer? Why? I don't understand. Why would you do that?"

"I'll keep my daughter safe even if you refuse to." He narrowed his eyes to slits. "I trusted you, but I don't trust you anymore."

"Lucas, stop. This is ridiculous. We don't need lawyers. I'd never do anything to hurt her. I love her as much as you do."

"No, you don't. You're too blinded by your love for Noah. You can't think straight." His words were bullets.

"I will not apologize for trying to keep my family together."

"We're not a family anymore. I'm warning you, Adrianne. This is serious. Don't push me." He grabbed her bag from my hands and marched into the house, leaving me standing alone in the driveway, stunned.

9

School didn't get any easier for Noah as the weeks went on. He wasn't making any friends, but I was pretty sure he wasn't trying. Making friends wasn't the only thing he didn't care about. He'd always been meticulous about his school work and an A-honor roll student, but he had no interest in his schoolwork either. I'd never had to be on him about his homework. The old Noah worked on his homework without any prompting or cajoling and took great pride in his work. This new Noah could care less.

His teachers started sending notes home about his lack of completion on projects and failing test scores. When I brought it to his attention, he said the material was hard, but he was lying. The stuff they were studying in math and English were things he did in his ninth-grade honors classes.

"Have you looked into whether or not they have a swim team at your school?" I asked that night as we sat watching the latest *Survivor* episode.

"No," he said without breaking his stare from the TV.

"Are you going to?"

I'd given up pressing him about doing things outside the

apartment but still nagged him about swimming. I couldn't let it go because he'd always been the happiest in a pool. I clung to the magic of the water as if it had the power to bring him back to life. He always said that the thing he loved most about swimming was how he didn't think of anything else from the moment his body was submerged in the water. He couldn't go more than two days without it. The water was his sanctuary, and if I could get him in it again, maybe it would begin to wash away his pain.

"What if we went to the YMCA just for fun? We could take Katie. She'd love that."

He burst out laughing. "You know she hates to swim."

Unlike Noah, she wouldn't even put her face in the water when she started swimming lessons. She kicked and screamed her way through every one we forced her to take. As soon as she was safe enough not to drown, we let her quit, but she loved watching Noah. She rarely missed a meet and loved sitting poolside waving the banners she spent hours creating.

"What if me and you went? It's been a long time since I went swimming. It might feel good."

He snorted. "Seriously? You're worse than Katie."

I threw a pillow at him. "So? Let's do it. It could still be fun. How about this weekend? If anything it'll get our pathetic asses out of the house."

He dropped his mouth in mock surprise. "You swore."

I smiled. "You're not the only one who's changed."

*****

I dug my suit out of my closet the next day while he was at

school. I hadn't worn it in years, and it was too big because I'd lost over thirty pounds. Some people buried their sorrow in food, but not me. I stopped eating as soon as Noah confessed. I felt sick all the time and just the thought of food made me nauseous. When I forced myself to eat, the food tasted like sawdust and within minutes, I exploded in the bathroom. I had to learn how to eat again, but my appetite had never returned to what it was before, and I did my best not to eat in public because sometimes my stomach still rejected food.

I splurged on a new suit to celebrate Noah getting back into the water. I was excited to show it to him when he got home from school, but instead of sitting down at the table for a cup of coffee like we usually did, he shuffled past me and headed for his bedroom. I waited a few minutes for him to come back out, but he didn't, so I walked down the hallway and knocked on his door.

No answer.

I knocked again.

Still no answer.

"Noah, can I come in?"

"Just go away. I want to be left alone."

Something in his voice was off.

"I'm coming in," I said as I pushed open the door.

He was curled up on his bed, laying on his side. I sat down next to him.

"What's wrong?" I placed my hand on his shoulder.

He shrugged my hand off him. "I don't want to talk about it."

"Did something happen at school today?"

"I said I didn't want to talk about it." He scooted further away.

"Okay, fine, but I'm here if you need me," I said.

I left him alone, but my worry grew when he refused to come out for dinner. Images of the days he used to stay locked in his room flashed through my mind while I put away the dishes. I couldn't help but remember why he holed himself up back then. I kept telling myself it was different—something was wrong, but not that. It couldn't be. Despite what I told myself, I couldn't leave him alone and walked into his room uninvited after the dishes were put away.

"I can't help you if I don't know what's going on," I announced.

He hadn't moved from his position on the bed. "You can't help me."

"Let me try." I grabbed his arms and pulled him up. He sat back against the headboard, pulling his knees up to his chest. His eyes were red and puffy.

"They know," he said.

I didn't have to ask what he was referring to.

"Who knows?" I asked.

"People at school."

My heart thudded. "How do you know that?"

"This guy, Spencer, he's like the biggest jock at the school. I told you about him before. Remember? The football star?"

"Right. The moron who's dating three girls at the same time?"

He gave me a half-smile. "That's him. Anyway, he's in my P.E. class. Today when we were going out onto the field, he grabbed me, and called me a sick perv." The tips of his ears were red.

"That guy is a jerk. You said so yourself. He makes fun of everyone. I guess today was your turn, and he decided to call you a pervert. I'm sure he has no idea about you."

He didn't look convinced.

"Look, there's always a guy in high school who gets his kicks out of bashing other people. And unfortunately, it's usually the guy everyone likes. I was always so proud of you because no matter how well you did in sports, you never turned into a jerk. A lot of guys aren't like that."

"I don't know. I felt like he was telling the truth, like he knew something. I could see it in his eyes." He chewed on his fingernails, whittled down to nubs. It was a new habit he picked up while he was away.

"I think you might be making a bigger deal out of it than it is. You got lucky in school, honey. You always had it easy. Most of us don't make it through without some kind of torture. Middle school was awful for me."

"You got picked on?"

"I had my share. And believe me, girls are way crueler than guys." I could already see the difference in how Katie was treated in elementary school versus what it'd been like for Noah. The girls had been grouped into cliques since kindergarten and it got worse each year.

"What happened to you?" Noah asked.

"You really want to know?"

He nodded.

I hadn't talked to my kids about what it was like for me in middle school. I always thought I'd have the conversation with Katie once she reached middle school. I never expected to be having it with him.

"There's no way to win when you're a girl. You're ridiculed for developing too early, but if you're too late, then they call you a freak. I was one of those girls who developed early and grew curves long before anyone else. It was so embarrassing, and I hated it. I had to wear a bra in fourth grade and everyone snapped it, even the girls. And then, in sixth grade, you have to start taking showers after gym class. It was awful." I shuddered at the memory.

"It doesn't sound so awful."

"Oh, believe me, it was, and it got worse. One day during gym class, I got my period." I paused. "Is this too much for you to hear about your mom? Am I totally grossing you out?"

He shook his head. "Keep going. I want to hear it."

"Okay, if you say so, but consider yourself warned." It was the first time in a long time he seemed interested in what I was saying, so I continued even though my cheeks flushed with embarrassment. "I didn't know what to do. It was my first one, and nobody's prepared for their first one. I stuffed my shorts with toilet paper and went back to class, but on my way back to class, my bloody toilet paper fell out. Right there in the middle of the hallway. It was mortifying and I couldn't deny it was me because it plopped right down between my legs on the floor. It was just like in the movies, everyone pointing and laughing hysterically. They called me Bloody Mary for the rest of the school year."

"God, Mom, that's awful."

"See, I told you you're not the only one. Feel better now?"

He laughed. "Sadly, I do."

"Well, come on, then. I want to show you the new swimming suit I got for the weekend." I yanked him up and led him back into the apartment, happy to have averted a crisis.

*****

I was busy typing the transcription file due by the end of the day when Noah staggered through the door. His t-shirt was ripped and coated in dirt. His jeans were grass-stained and smeared with blood. He hung his head and held his shoulder with arms covered in bruises and red marks. I jumped up.

"Noah, what happened?"

He looked up and smiled, revealing a mouthful of blood. His entire face was covered in angry welts. A cut above his eyebrow revealed the pearly-white flesh of his forehead. His right eye was blackened. His left one swollen shut.

"It's happening again," he said before collapsing on the carpet.

I rushed to his side. There was so much blood. His eyes were closed.

"Noah, who did this? What happened?" I shrieked.

He just shook his head and moaned.

"Tell me. You have to tell me! Open your eyes! Open your eyes!" I shook him back and forth, whipping his head around. It couldn't be happening again. It had to be something else. He hadn't moved, barely flinched. "Noah! Noah!"

Nothing.

His head rolled onto the carpet. I let him go and jumped up, running through the apartment looking for my phone. I found it on the bathroom counter. I tapped out 911 while I raced back into the living room.

"911. What is your emergency?"

"Please, my son has been beat up. He's unconscious."

"Is he there with you now?"

"Yes."

"Is he breathing?"

"Yes." Despite his unresponsiveness, his chest moved up and down rhythmically, but he was in so much pain, he moaned with each breath. "Please hurry."

"What's your address, ma'am?"

"2819 West Keystone Avenue."

"Mom?" Noah looked up at me with one eye. His other swollen shut.

I knelt next to him. "Honey, I'm sorry. I didn't mean to freak out. I'm here. I'm right here," I whispered, cradling the phone on my shoulder. "The ambulance is coming soon."

"I don't need an ambulance," he coughed.

The operator broke in. "Okay, it looks like we can have a unit there in about twenty minutes."

"Twenty minutes? What? No. Not twenty minutes. You have to come now." I'd never heard of such a thing, having to wait for an ambulance. "This is an emergency."

"I'm sorry, but that's the soonest we can have someone to you."

There was no way. I wasn't waiting twenty minutes. I hung up. I scrambled through the house, gathering up things as fast as I could and throwing them into a bag. Noah still hadn't moved from his spot in front of the door, but at least he was conscious.

"Noah, honey, we have to get you to the hospital. I don't want to wait for the ambulance. I'm going to need your help to get you downstairs and in the car. Do you think you can walk?"

He nodded. I wrapped my arm around him and helped pull him to his feet. We shuffled through our door and down the hallway. I breathed a sigh of relief that none of our neighbors were around. Noah leaned into me for support in the elevator.

"Who did this?" I asked.

"You already know," he said.

*****

I held his hand while he slept. He'd been asleep since they wheeled him back from X-rays. His collarbone was broken and so were two of his ribs from where they'd kicked him while he was down. I'd gotten the story out in pieces on the drive to the hospital. Spencer and two of his friends had jumped him two blocks from our house while he was walking to school. One of them had a baseball bat and they'd beaten him with it. He needed twenty-seven stitches to connect his eyebrow back to his skin, five on his chin, and eight on the deep gash on his knee. They'd pumped him full of morphine to help with the pain.

I was glad he was asleep because I couldn't stop crying and didn't want him to see it. Two months. It'd only been two months and here we were again. What was I going to do?

A knock at the door startled me. I quickly wiped my face with my sleeve and rearranged my face as a short woman walked through the door carrying an iPad. She walked around to the other side of Noah's bed so she could see my face.

"I'm Dr. Phillips, but you can call me Lisa," she said. "I'm one of the clinical psychologists at the hospital. You must be Noah's mom?"

She was the opposite of Dr. Park. Whereas she always looked put together, Dr. Phillips's long hair was haphazardly pulled up in a bun with a pen sticking through it. Her clothes were loose and slung low on her hips. She had a white doctor coat on but was missing the stethoscope.

I nodded, wrestling with the emotions in my throat. "I'm Adrianne."

"I'm so sorry that you're going through this," she said. "I know you've been through a lot today, but I was wondering if I might be able to talk to Noah alone? It's standard procedure for whenever a child comes into the hospital with injuries like this."

She had to make sure I wasn't the one who hurt him. I wanted to cry and laugh at the same time. I'd been the one to ask parents to leave so we could assess the situation, but I'd never been on the receiving end. It felt awful even though I knew she was just doing her job.

"Sure," I said.

"Why don't you step out into the waiting room? See if you can't get yourself a cup of coffee?" Her voice was kind. Her eyes gentle.

I got up and headed for the waiting room. Maybe it was better that she questioned him alone. I wasn't sure I could hear the details of what they'd done to him. I spotted Lucas sitting in a chair in the corner as far away as he could get from the young man throwing up in a plastic bag. He stood when he saw me and shoved his hands in his pockets, looking nervous.

"They told me about his injuries. Sounds pretty rough," he said, shuffling back and forth on his feet.

"He doesn't look good."

He reached under his seat, pulled out a Starbucks mug, and handed it to me.

"Thanks." I took it and sat in the chair next to his. "There's a psychologist meeting with him now."

"Why's he meeting with a psychologist?"

"Don't pretend you care," I snapped.

He balked as if I slapped him in the face.

"Why are you here?" I asked.

"You called me," he huffed.

"Right. Because I called you. Not because you actually give a shit what happens to him. What are you going to do when he walks out of here? You going to hug him? Ask him if he's okay? No, you're going to stare at him like he's some kind of freak and make him feel worse than he already does."

"I … I …"

"Tell me I'm wrong. Go on. Tell me." I glared at him.

"I …" He opened his mouth, then shut it again.

"You don't even care if he dies." I spat out the words.

"That's not true."

But it was. I could see it in his eyes. He was just like everybody else.

"Just go." I pointed toward the exit.

"Are you serious?" He looked shocked.

"Yes, go."

He didn't put up a fight or argue to stay. He walked out of the waiting room without looking back. I seethed with anger. All of this was his fault. If he hadn't made me choose between abandoning Noah and living with them, we never would've moved to the new apartment. Noah wouldn't have been walking to school because even though they only lived a few blocks away, they were zoned within a different school district, and he would've had to take the bus. He'd be living in the same house with Katie, the only person who brought him joy in his life right now, but Lucas had taken that away too.

I'd been on the verge of a breakdown and giving up, but my anger toward Lucas gave me strength. I let it fill me, pulling me away from the devastation threatening to overtake me. I needed someone to hate, or I might fall apart. This time, I didn't know if I could put myself back together again. I sucked back my tears, set my jaw, and sat up straighter.

I got up, filled with determination, and walked back into Noah's room. Dr. Phillips was gone. He was sitting on the bed, his left arm in a strange sling to keep his collarbone in place. He was in a fresh hospital gown. His other arm clutched his stomach as he stared into space, eyes wide and unblinking. I wanted to hug him but didn't want to hurt him. He'd never looked as fragile as he did at this moment, not even when he was an infant and I'd stared at him in his bassinet while he slept.

"Hey," I said softly.

He didn't look up, just kept staring straight ahead. He looked like he didn't hear me.

"How'd it go with the psychologist?" I asked tentatively.

Still nothing.

"Noah?" I stepped in front of him and waved my hand in front of his eyes. Nothing. Not a flinch. "I'm going to see if I can track down the psychologist."

I didn't have to look far. She was hovering at the nurses' station, writing down orders.

"Excuse me." I tapped her on the shoulder, and she turned around. "Sorry to bother you."

"Don't worry about it," she said. "I was just making notes in Noah's chart."

"What's wrong with him?" I asked.

"He's in shock. It's terrifying to be attacked the way he was. His pupils are dilated, which suggests he was most likely knocked unconscious during the fight. The doctors have also ordered a CT scan to make sure there isn't any swelling in his brain. They're going to keep him in the hospital overnight for observation. The police should be here shortly to take his statement. I'll be with him during the interview to try to help him through it and keep it from being too overwhelming. You're welcome to be there too. Do you have any idea why he was attacked?"

Her eyes were filled with such compassion and care. Her voice was gentle and filled with concern. I didn't want to tell her. As soon as she knew the reason they beat him, all of it would disappear. She'd look at him the same way everyone else did.

"I have no idea why they attacked him," I said.

10

"He hasn't left his room for three days. He just lays in his bed and stares at the ceiling. He won't eat. He doesn't sleep. I don't know what to do," I cried.

I swore when I left Marsh I'd never talk to Dr. Park again after the way she handled his discharge, but I had nowhere else to turn.

"Have you thought about getting in contact with the psychologist at the hospital? Maybe he needs to be institutionalized," she said.

"Like put in the psych ward?"

"Yes, it might help stabilize him."

"I'm afraid that it would make him worse." Locking him up in a hospital with no access to the outside world was too much, and he'd spent enough of his adolescence institutionalized.

"Have you thought about moving?" she asked.

"We just moved and even if we moved again, what difference will it make? This will follow him to the next school. What are we supposed to do? Keep running from place to place?"

There was no escaping what he did. It was attached to us like a malignant tumor. Noah told the police he didn't know his attackers, but I knew he wasn't telling the truth. He'd told me in the car that it was Spencer and his friends. He also said he didn't remember much of the assault because he hit his head and was knocked out for most of it. I hoped that part was true, that he'd been unconscious while they broke his bones.

I felt stupid for believing no one would find out about him. I don't know why I hadn't done it before, but I googled his name while we were in the hospital. It wasn't difficult to find him. He was listed as a sex offender on the third page of results, but that wasn't the most disturbing thing I found. Someone had created a Facebook page in his name: *Noah Coates (Baby Raper).* It'd been created around the time he got convicted, back when we lived in Buffalo Grove. Recently, it'd sprung back to life with a vengeance. I had stayed away from reading any of the comments in the media during his trial but couldn't stop myself this time. I scrolled through hundreds and hundreds of hate-filled comments, many of them coupled with death threats. I couldn't believe it was happening again. Not again.

The police must've found it too, which explained why they didn't follow up after the hospital despite how concerned they were initially. They had bombarded him with questions. What did he remember about the attack? What was he doing in the moments before it happened? Did he know of anyone who would want to hurt him? They'd promised to get to the bottom of it. Find out who did it and arrest them. We hadn't heard a peep from them since. Nothing.

He'd been beaten and broken. Not once, but twice. He'd been ridiculed, shamed, chased out of his home, and school. Lost all his friends. His dad. Anything he ever cared about. He'd served time, registered as a sex offender, and followed all their rules. When was enough going to be enough?

The first time around, I was devastated as our lives were destroyed and filled with so much shame and guilt I couldn't do anything except heap their hate on my shoulders. But it was different now. There wasn't anything left for them to take. They couldn't destroy anything else. It was all gone.

*****

"What about homeschooling?" Dr. Park asked on our daily check-in call. I'd gone to her for help but she had the same grasping-for-straws tone in her voice that I had in my gut.

"How am I supposed to homeschool him when he can't use the Internet?"

"Sometimes the law will make an exception, and this is certainly one of the cases where they should. I can contact his probation officer and let him know about his situation. Maybe if I talk to them, they'll allow it. There will be strict rules for his use and you'll have to monitor him closely, but I've had other clients who were able to do it. There are all kinds of online programs available through the school district."

I gave her all the information she needed, and she promised to start working on it as soon as we hung up. I was pacing the living room when there was a knock at the door. It took me off guard. Nobody visited us. I opened it to find Lucas standing on our welcome mat. I hadn't seen or talked to him since our argument in the hospital waiting room.

"What are you doing here?" I asked, not bothering to invite him in.

"I wanted to see how you guys are doing." He rubbed his hands through his hair.

"We're fine," I said, my voice clipped.

"Can I see him?"

"Why?" I put my hands on my hips.

He shrugged. "I want to know if he's okay."

"Well, he's not. Not even close." I glared at him.

He let out a deep sigh. "Adrianne, please, let me in. Don't do this."

"Seeing you is only going to hurt him. I'm not going to let you keep hurting him."

I was done letting people hurt my son. He'd been punished enough.

"I'm trying." He looked down at his feet.

"No, you're not." I kept my voice low so Noah wouldn't hear. I stepped out into the hallway with him, shutting the door closed behind me. "You've done nothing."

"Really? Nothing? I didn't sell my house? Move to this shitty-ass part of town? I don't drive an hour each way just to go to work? I didn't give up my entire life so he wouldn't have to go to jail? I haven't drained my retirement or rearranged my whole world so he could have a life? But, you're right—you've done it all." His nose flared in and out.

Anger surged through me. "You didn't have a choice. Don't act like you did any of it because you wanted to. You did it out of obligation." I took my finger and plunged it into his chest, pushing him backward. "You haven't told him you loved him since it happened. Not once have you uttered those words. You took away your love the minute he didn't fit into the box you'd put him in."

"Didn't fit into a box? Christ, you act like he failed a test at school. He's a fuckin' child molester." He spat out the word.

"It doesn't mean he's a monster. He has a problem." My voice shook.

"Stop saying that!" he yelled. "Do you know how many times you've said, that like somehow I don't get it? I'm the one who gets it. You're the one that doesn't understand."

"What? Enlighten me. What exactly is it that I don't understand?" My rage consumed me. I wanted to claw his eyes out, pummel him with my fists, anything to make him hurt.

He shook his head wildly. "You don't want to hear it. You act like you do, but you don't. You don't want to talk about it for real. You talk about what he did like he robbed some bank and went off to treatment to learn how not to steal again. You're in la-la land about it. Always have been."

"That's not true. Just because I still love him doesn't mean I'm not in reality."

Loving him wasn't something to be ashamed of. I'd never apologize for it.

"Bullshit. You can tell that to yourself all you want, but it doesn't make it true." He gestured at the door behind me. "What he's got, what's wrong with him—it doesn't go away. There's something broken inside him. Something you can't fix. Even if you want to. Even if he wants to."

"You can't say that. How do you know that? You don't know

that."

"You want to know how I know?" He leaned into me, his face inches from mine. "Because I'm a man, and men aren't supposed to have thoughts or fantasies about touching little girls. It's sick and disgusting." His eyes were on fire.

The wind in my fight left me. The lights in the hallway were too bright. Lucas's face too close.

"Just leave. Go away. I don't want you here."

He raised his voice. "See, that's what I mean. You say you want to talk about things, but you don't. You want to talk about the delusion you've created rather than reality. You run away anytime it gets close to the truth."

"I'm not running away. I just don't think we should be having this conversation in the hallway." I was spent. My fury was gone and replaced with tears.

"Where would you like to have it, then?"

"In our house. The one you kicked me and your son out of." I stepped back and shut the door in his face.

HIM(THEN)

I wish Mom wouldn't visit. I shouldn't feel that way, but I do. She makes me remember home and life out there. It's too dangerous to think about the world outside these walls because it makes it harder to be here. I have to pretend like nothing else exists to survive. It's the only way to make it through. I want to tell her not to come anymore but it would devastate her, and I've already caused her enough pain. It hurts to even look at her.

She smiles through every visit, but the smile on her face is a lie. There's no hiding the pain etched on her face, and her eyes look like she hasn't slept in years. She loses more weight every time I see her. She never stops talking when she's here. It's like she's afraid of the silence.

Everything is different when the parents visit. Staff lets us go outside and walk around the yard without the guards. Our parents eat lunch with us, and it's the meal I look forward to every week because it's the only one resembling real food. Most of our meals are slop—scoops of goo that they plop on our plates like dog food. But when the parents are here we get burgers or pizza. It still tastes like cafeteria food but it's a thousand times better than what we usually get. Most of the parents don't eat but we scarf it down. They even let us have seconds, and we never get seconds. Everyone's happy during lunch, even the kids who don't have parents visiting because they still get to eat with us.

Last week I told her she can't cry and hold on to me when she leaves. The others are going to start noticing, and they'll make fun of me about it. They can't see me as a momma's boy. She looked like I'd slapped her when I told her but she agreed to a quick hug and promised there'd be no tears. I could tell how hard it was for her today when she told me good-bye, but she didn't cry even though she wanted to. The tears were in her throat, but she didn't let them move down her cheeks. She hugged me and then let go quickly. It hurt her but she always puts my needs above hers. That's just the kind of mom she is, but sometimes I think it'd be easier to be like the kids who don't have anybody to care about them.

11

Dr. Park arranged for Noah to attend school online. I had to pay for all the monitoring equipment and programs, but I didn't care. It was worth it. Noah perked up for a second when he found out he didn't have to go back to school, but quickly slipped back into his depressed state. It was just like the days before his confession. He went days without a shower, and I had to force him to do it. He barely ate. I tried everything, all his favorite meals. I even made a batch of my homemade chicken soup, but he didn't take more than a few bites before pushing it away.

The walls of our apartment were closing in on me. It'd been two weeks since we left the hospital, and he hadn't stepped foot out of the apartment, not even to get the mail or bring the laundry down to the laundry room for me. I could've left the apartment and he probably wouldn't notice my absence, but I was compelled to be with him in his pain. I didn't want to leave him feel alone.

Since I wasn't leaving the apartment, I couldn't get Katie from school, so Lucas dropped her off on her visiting days. Lucas and I had only spoken about the logistics with Katie since our confrontation in the hallway, and we talked to each other like robots when we did. Most of the time he didn't even bring her into the building. He just texted from the curb and I ran down to get her. Even Katie couldn't snap Noah out of his trancelike state. He wouldn't let her touch him. He pushed her away, saying it hurt his ribs too much. It might be true, but I doubted it.

I was on the phone with Dr. Park constantly, asking her advice about what to do about him. She suggested inviting one of his friends from Marsh to come visit Noah for the weekend, and I rejected the idea without a second thought. That part of his life was over, and I didn't want him making friends with those kinds of kids. It seemed hypocritical, but Noah wasn't like anyone else in treatment. I went to all the education and parent support groups while he was at Marsh and I'd heard all of their stories. Noah's case was the least serious. He was like the kid in treatment for smoking pot a few times surrounded by kids who shot heroin.

But Dr. Park wouldn't let the idea go. She brought it up every time we talked. She thought it was a great idea because of the powerful social pressure during adolescence.

"Think about it for a second—would he want his peers to see him this way?" she asked. "He's not going to lay around on the couch all day if there's someone else there to see it."

I didn't like referring to the kids from Marsh as his peers, but she had a point. At least, I wouldn't have to be worried about his anonymity if the kid was from Marsh. It might be good for him not to have to constantly censor himself to make sure he didn't give anything away about his history. It took me a few more days to think about it, but eventually I agreed.

Dr. Park suggested Rick come for the visit since he was only a year younger than Noah and only lived two hours away. They'd been in treatment at the same time, and she explained that went through a similar process.

"What'd he do?" I asked.

I didn't want someone who committed a violent sex crime in my home. During group, I listened in horror about kids who'd committed unspeakable crimes against other kids. They were the types of offenders who scared me—the predatory, sadistic sex ones. They were the worst kind and the most dangerous. They took pleasure from inflicting pain on others just for the enjoyment of watching them suffer. There was no way I was letting one of them into my house.

I wanted a kid like Noah. I was only comfortable with the visit if he was someone like him, who had insight into the wrongness of his actions and was trying to change. I had to know something about Rick's history before I could let him in my home.

"You know I can't disclose confidential client information," she said.

"Is he dangerous? Can you at least tell me that?"

"I can tell you this—he's not violent. He's a boy who was going through puberty and very curious about girls. He made some poor choices due to his lack of impulse control and poor social skills."

I agreed despite the fluttering of doubt inside me. Dr. Park arranged it for us, and I appreciated not having to do it myself. Rick lived with his grandmother, and she didn't drive, so the plan was for Rick to take the bus to the metro station in downtown Chicago and I would pick him up from there.

“Are you kidding me? I can’t believe you did that without asking me.” Noah’s eyes flared with anger when I told him we were having Rick over to spend the night on Friday.

It was his first emotional response since he’d gotten out of the hospital. Even if he hated me for making him do it, at least he was feeling something. It was better than him walking around like he was half-dead.

“He doesn’t live far away from us, and it might be helpful for you to have a friend. Dr. Park thinks it’s a good idea. She’s worried about how isolated you are,” I explained it exactly as she instructed me to. She warned me he might not be open to the idea given his current emotional state. “I know you’ve got to be lonely. It’s—”

He interrupted me. “I’m not lonely. I don’t need a friend.”

There was no way that was true.

“We can give it a try and see how it goes. Dr. Park said the two of you got along well at Marsh.”

“Just because we got along doesn’t mean we’re friends.” He scowled.

“It’s going to be nice. You’ll see. We’re going to pick him up in the city, and I thought we could have dinner while we were there. Then, on Saturday, you guys can go to a movie or something.”

He rolled his eyes. “Whatever. This sucks.”

He sulked the entire ride to the station, but he’d showered before we left and put on something other than sweatpants for the first time since the hospital. He wore the skinny jeans he picked out a few weeks before, but hadn’t worn, and one of his vintage Beatles t-shirts that he’d picked up years ago at one of our favorite flea markets.

Unlike Noah, Rick had a phone, and texted us when he arrived. We pulled up along Fifty-Third Avenue, and as soon as Noah pointed him out on the curb, I second-guessed what I'd done.

He was short, much shorter than Noah, with deep-set green eyes and heavy dark brown eyebrows coupled with an expression that warned, "Don't mess with me." He was dressed in black from his t-shirt all the way down to his black combat boots. Even his fingernails were painted black. Blond roots poked through his dark hair that made his already pale complexion look pasty.

He slid into the backseat.

"What's up, bro?" he asked Noah.

"Nothing," Noah responded without looking at him.

"I'm Adrianne, Noah's mom. Nice to meet you." I smiled back at him in the rearview mirror. No response. He didn't acknowledge I'd spoken. I pulled away from the curb and headed to the restaurant. They were both silent as we drove. Rick tapped away on his phone the entire ride, his eyes glued to the screen. At the restaurant, he pulled it out again and set it on the table.

"Have you played the new Assassin's Creed?" he asked.

Noah shook his head. "No video games for me." He shot me a pointed look.

"Damn, you're totally missing out. It's badass. Check this out." He opened up a screen, and Noah leaned closer to peer at it with him.

Rick didn't flinch when he swore in front of me. Noah's old friends never would've dreamed of swearing in front of me. It was an implied social understanding that kids didn't swear in front of parents. It was unnerving.

Noah joined in, tapping away on the screen. "That's so cool."

"What about Limbo? You downloaded it yet?" Rick asked.

"Dude, I don't even have a phone."

"No way, are you serious? That's like child abuse or something."

Didn't he know he wasn't supposed to have a phone either? At least not a smartphone, and there was no way either of them would use a flip phone.

Before I knew it, they were engaged in a battle on the video game Rick downloaded. I sat back and watched them, realizing how long it'd been since I'd seen Noah interact with a teenager in a real-world setting. To all outside appearances, they looked like normal teenagers. It made my eyes film.

They played all through dinner, and I didn't stop them. It didn't matter that they weren't talking to each other outside of whatever was going on in the game because they were having fun. Noah was animated and lively. He devoured his chicken Alfredo pasta. Rick ate the steak he ordered from the most expensive spot on the menu, but I let it go. It was worth the expense to see my son alive even if his friend was incredibly rude.

*****

I was thrilled about the visit despite how odd and socially awkward Rick was. He didn't have any manners; didn't say thank you for anything the whole time he was with us. He swore as if it was nothing. His vocabulary extended far beyond the soft cuss words. He dropped f-bombs without caring. He was someone I would've steered Noah away from in the past—pointed him in the direction of making other friends, and warned him about the importance of making good choices in who he spent his time with—but we no longer lived by the same rules.

His presence energized Noah, and that's what I cared about. The other things paled in comparison. What if I got Noah a phone? At least if he had a phone, he could text Rick and other friends he might meet. It was only a matter time before Noah broke the ice at school and started making friends. He'd definitely need a phone then because texting was the primary way teenagers communicated. Noah and his friends used to text each other when they were in the same room. Having a phone would allow him to play video games with them too. He might not be able to use a console, but if he had a phone, he could play on it like they did all weekend.

As I hurried through my grocery shopping, I considered talking to Dr. Park about getting Noah a phone. There had to be a way to set up monitoring on the phone like we did on the computer for his online school. But what if she said no? Should I just do it without asking permission? He couldn't go to jail for having a smartphone, could he? It felt foreign to think about breaking the rules. I'd never broken any kind of a law. I didn't know how people broke rules. I'd always been that way. It wasn't because I hated getting into trouble even though I did, but there was something fundamental inside of me that felt obligated to do the right thing simply because it was the right thing.

I missed talking to Lucas. We used to sit down and hash out the pros and cons of each big parenting decision until we reached an agreement. He was always able to point out things I couldn't see and vice versa. Those days were gone. We didn't even talk about decisions with Katie anymore, and she was the easy one. He did what he wanted with her when she was at his house, and I did what I wanted with her when she was at mine.

I used to be afraid we'd reach this point—the place where we'd moved so far away from each other that we couldn't come back together. But now that it had happened, it wasn't nearly as awful as I imagined it'd be. The person I knew and loved was gone. I didn't want to get close to the new Lucas who'd taken his place. We were fundamentally different. Maybe we always had been.

I pushed aside the thoughts about Lucas like I always did. I didn't have the emotional energy to deal with our crumbling marriage on top of everything else. I would work it out once I got through this year with Noah. Until then, I was going to have to deal with things as they were.

The weekend had renewed my faith that we could learn how to live in this new life even though it was a life neither of us wanted. I smiled to myself, wondering what Noah would say if I told him I was considering breaking the rules and getting him a phone. I hurried to pick up the last items on my grocery list and get back home so I could make us dinner.

I walked in the door expecting to find him sitting on the couch, but the couch was empty, and the TV turned off.

"Noah?" I called out.

Nothing.

I put the bags on the counter and walked down the hallway to his room. I lifted my hand to knock when I heard him retching. I threw open the door. He was leaning over his bed, spewing violently on the floor. It was covered in puddles of puke. The stench made me gag.

"Get up, get into the bathroom!" I yelled, instinctively covering my mouth and nose with my hand.

He kept hurling on the floor, clutching his stomach. I ran and pulled him up. He spewed vomit as I shoved him into the hallway. His movements were sluggish and slow. I dragged him to the bathroom. He fell toward the toilet, wrapping his arms around it with his head halfway in. I rubbed his back while he heaved. He didn't take his head out of the toilet even after the heaving stopped.

"Why didn't you get to the bathroom when you felt sick?" I asked. It was going to take forever to clean up the mess he'd made.

"It happened so fast. I felt fine and then all of a sudden, I was throwing up. I think I've got food poisoning." He let out a deep moan.

"What'd you eat?"

He heaved again before he could respond. He moaned with each convulsion. I grabbed a washcloth from the sink, wet it, and held it on his neck.

He pushed my hand away. "Mom, you've got to get out of here. I have to sit on the toilet too."

I scrambled up, shutting the door tightly behind me. The smell of vomit surrounded me. I held back the urge to gag. I hated vomit. Always had. When Noah was little and got the stomach flu, I used to throw up with him because of the sounds and smell. It got easier after a while, but it'd been a long time since either of them had been this sick. I took a few deep breaths to settle my stomach.

I went into the kitchen and filled a large bucket full of water, waiting to squeeze in the soap until the water was scalding. I started on the hallway walls. He'd splattered them with brown on his way to the bathroom. There were more spots on the carpet. I breathed through my mouth while I scrubbed them and they came up easily since they hadn't had time to settle. The sounds coming from the bathroom were awful. I was grateful not to be in there.

It didn't take me long to finish the hallway, but his bedroom was a different story. I didn't know where to begin. It was a disaster. I grabbed plastic garbage bags and balled up all his bedding, stuffing it inside.

"Noah, I'm going to run your bedding down to the laundry room," I called out before heading downstairs.

I wasn't used to not doing laundry in my home. It'd been two decades since I'd had to leave to do laundry. At least the unit had laundry facilities on site. When I got back upstairs, I pulled clean sheets and blankets out of the hallway closet and made a bed for him on the couch. I took the waste basket in my bedroom and emptied it, then washed it, and placed it next to the couch. I had a feeling I would be spending most of the night emptying and cleaning out his bucket. I'd only had food poisoning once in my twenties, and I threw up for two days. It was brutal.

I knocked on the bathroom door. "Honey, are you okay?"

"Yes." His voice was weak.

"Are you ready to come out? I made a bed up for you on the couch."

He opened the door, and the foul smell of diarrhea assaulted me. He shuffled down the hallway and fell onto the couch.

I didn't bother cleaning the bathroom. I would wait to attack it until he felt better. I moved into his room. I had never seen so much vomit. It covered both sides of the floor by his bed. I wished

I hadn't sold my Bissel carpet cleaner in the moving sale, because I had no idea how I was going to get it up. Even if I cleaned up the puke, the smell was going to stay.

I started scrubbing the floor by the right side of the bed. I noticed an empty pill bottle next to one of the piles of puke. I picked it up and twirled it between my fingers to read the label. It was Noah's prescription for Percocet. A rush of horror burned my insides. I clutched the bottle against my chest, stifling a scream, and walked back into the living room. Noah was curled on his side, eyes closed.

"Sit up." The anger in my voice surprised me.

He opened his eyes. His pupils were dots, the lids heavy. His face pale.

I threw the pill bottle at him. He moved to catch it, but his reaction time was slow. It fell on the couch next to him.

"What did you do?" My voice quivered.

"Nothing."

"Don't lie to me. Don't you dare lie to me."

He hung his head.

"Did you take these?"

He nodded.

"How many?"

He shrugged.

"How many?"

"Whatever was left? I don't know. I didn't count."

I picked it back up. It was empty. They'd given him twenty pills, and we hadn't refilled the prescription. I didn't know how many he'd taken before today. I hadn't monitored them. It never occurred to me that I needed to. I trusted him to take them when he needed to because of his pain. He said he stopped taking them after a few days because he didn't like how they made him feel. How many did that leave?

"Come on. Get up. We need to go the hospital." I yanked the blanket off him.

"Mom, no, please. I can't go back to the hospital. I'm okay. Really."

"You need to have a doctor check you out. Pump your stomach."

"There's nothing left in my stomach to pump." He rubbed his forehead.

I sat on the couch next to him, holding my head in my hands. My chest hurt. My head swirled. The smell of sickness surrounded me.

"What were you trying to do?" I asked.

"What do you mean?"

"You know exactly what I mean."

"I don't know." He laid his head back down on the couch. "My head is throbbing."

"Were you trying to get high or ... or were you ..."

My words hung in the air.

"I just didn't want to feel anything." His eyes filled with desperation. "Please, don't make me go to the hospital. Dad will come, and it'll be awful. I hate all the doctors and that shrink will talk to me again. Please. I'm fine. I swear I'm fine. I learned my lesson. Please, Mom, I'm begging you."

I gave in and didn't take him to the hospital. I stayed up with him all night instead. He stopped dry-heaving somewhere around three in the morning. I made him drink water and eventually, he kept it down. I moved on to Gatorade, forcing him to take small sips. I didn't sleep at all. I checked on him every few minutes while he slept to make sure he kept breathing.

I didn't know if I was doing the right thing. It'd been two years since I'd been confident in a parenting decision, but I did know that I didn't fail him in this moment of desperation like I'd done before. I would never forgive myself for how I handled his confession. At least this time, I gave him what he needed.

He was in so much pain, and I didn't know how to stop it. I couldn't shake the feeling that Lucas held the key. My love for him wasn't enough. He needed his dad.

12

Noah was worse than he'd been before Rick's visit. He sat on the couch still as a statue, staring at the blank TV screen. He was back to not eating. He said it was because his stomach was recovering, but I didn't believe him. I didn't have any experience with not trusting him. None. He adhered to the same moral code as me. He followed the rules because that's what you were supposed to do.

I had to get Lucas to talk to Noah. I couldn't hold him up on my own anymore. It had been weeks since he invited us to their house and he'd made it clear we weren't welcome to come by unannounced. But whenever I asked, he made up some trivial excuse to keep us from coming. It took some coaxing, but he finally agreed to have us over for dinner and a movie the following night.

I waited until Katie and Noah were settled in front of the TV before I motioned for Lucas to follow me into the kitchen where he could keep one eye on Noah at all times while we talked. His face hardened and he folded his arms across his chest as he leaned against the counter.

"What's going on?" he asked.

"We need to talk." I lowered my voice. "Something happened with Noah."

He nodded, waiting for me to go on.

"You've got to talk to him. He needs you." I couldn't keep the desperation out of my voice.

His expression didn't change. I wasn't saying anything he hadn't heard many times before. I'd done everything I could think of to get him connect with Noah—begged, cried, bargained, screamed—but it never made a difference. He was as unmoved then as he was now.

"You can't tell him that I told you." Noah made me promise not to tell anyone what he'd done and I hated to betray his confidence, but it was the only way I could get Lucas to understand the seriousness of what we were dealing with.

"Okay." He looked confused.

"A few days ago, Noah took all his Percocet. I think he was trying to kill himself." I spoke quickly in case Katie came bouncing into the kitchen.

"What happened?" he asked, nonchalantly.

"He puked his brains out. It was awful. He begged me not to take him to the hospital, so I didn't. I don't know if I made the right choice or not. I have no idea what I'm doing anymore. I don't know how to help him, and I'm afraid of losing him. You've got to talk to him." I choked on the sobs caught in my throat.

He frowned. "I don't know if I can do that. I don't know what I'd say."

"Didn't you hear me? I said he tried to kill himself. He might die. Don't you care if he dies?" I couldn't keep the hysteria out of my voice.

"Of course I care if he dies." He pretended to act insulted.

"I don't know why I try. Why I even bother to come to you." My shoulders shook with silent sobs. He didn't reach out to hold me, or offer a hand of comfort like he would've done in the past. I'd become so enmeshed in his mind with Noah that he couldn't touch me either.

"I guess I could talk to him. Just tell me what you want me to say."

"I want you to tell him that you still love him and you're sorry for how you've treated him. I don't care if you mean it. Just say it. He needs to hear you say it. Please, Lucas, I'm begging you. Just pretend. Look at him and pretend he's the six-year-old boy you used to adore."

"Fine, I'll do it," he said and walked back into the living room looking like he was walking into a pit of snakes. "Noah, can I talk to you for a second?"

Noah perked up immediately, shocked that he'd spoken to him directly. "Sure," he said. His eyes lit up with excitement.

He leaped to his feet and turned around to give me a wide smile as he followed Lucas into the guest bedroom. They shut the door behind them.

I took his spot next to Katie. She nuzzled up under my arm and wrapped herself around me.

"Is everything okay?" she asked sleepily. It was already past her bedtime.

I breathed a sigh of relief. "It's going to be."

I expected Noah to look happy when he came out of the bedroom, but instead, he looked stricken. Lucas's expression hadn't changed. It was the same stoic face he'd been wearing for two years. I hoped forcing him to tell Noah that he loved him would crumble his armor and make him remember what it felt like to love him. Maybe he didn't love him anymore, but at one time he did. More than anything else in the world.

"Let's go, Mom," Noah said.

"Um ... okay?" I looked toward Lucas. He shrugged.

I peeled Katie off of me, laying her back against the couch. She'd fallen asleep while we waited for Noah and Lucas. I kissed her on the top of her head, not wanting to wake her up.

"What did your dad want to talk to you about?" I asked Noah as soon as we were in the car.

He shrugged. "Nothing."

"Come on. You haven't had a conversation in months. Fill me in on the details." I tried not to sound too eager.

He shrugged. "He said everything he needed to say."

"Could you be a bit more cryptic, please?"

"I don't want to talk about it," he snapped.

He went to his room as soon as we got home and closed the door. I had a hard time falling asleep even after taking half of an Ambien. Nights had always been the worst for me and eventually, I'd had to rely on sleeping pills. I hadn't slept without them in a year.

*****

Bloodcurdling screams startled me awake. I bolted from my

bed, ran to Noah's room, and flung open the door. His bed was empty. Smooth and unused. I whipped open the closet door.

Nothing.

The screaming continued.

I rushed to the bathroom. Flicked on the light. Empty.

Other voices joined the shrieking.

"Call 911! Call 911!"

Terror gripped me. I was blind with fear as I stumbled toward the living room. The patio door was ajar. We never went out on the patio. Horror mounted with each step. I looked down.

Noah's lifeless body dangled from our balcony, tied by his bedroom sheets. Ice water shot through my veins. I raced to the edge and tried to pull him up. He was too heavy.

"Help me! My God, someone help me!" My screams grew louder.

Everything was in slow motion. My hands pulled, twisted. I couldn't move him. People yelled. Their words didn't reach me. Someone pounded at my door. I couldn't leave him. I had to hold him up.

"Please God, please God, please God."

A loud crash. Suddenly, someone was behind me, pushing me out of the way. "Move!"

Two men shoved me aside and pulled on the rope like they were engaged in a tug-of-war contest. They grunted as they pulled and got him up to the railing but couldn't lift him over. Another man jumped in, and they hoisted him over the rail, laying him down on the concrete. His body flopped like a dead fish. They flipped him on his back. His eyes bulged out of his head, wide open in shock and horror. His lips were blue. His mouth contorted into a grotesque half-smile. His chest wasn't moving.

I tried to untie the knot from around his neck. I couldn't. It was too tight. "Grab a knife from the kitchen!" I screamed.

One of the men left and quickly came back with a knife. I held the rope as far away from Noah's neck as I could. It barely moved. He tied it tight. Done it right.

The man's hand hesitated. "I'm afraid I'll cut him."

"Give it to me." The other one grabbed it and sliced the noose in one swift movement. It fell away.

I put my face down to his. Nothing. I tilted his head back, cleared his airway, and gave two breaths. Placed both hands on his chest and pushed.

"One, two, three, four five," I chanted out loud.

Breathe. One. Two. Check.

"One, two, three, four, five."

Breathe. One. Two. Check.

"One, two, three, four five."

Breathe. One. Two. Check.

Big black boots. Navy legs pushed me away. Arms and hands everywhere moving like madness around his body, pushing me further and further away toward the end of the balcony. My heart hammered so loudly it echoed in my head. There was a sea of movement around me.

They pulled out the laryngoscope to intubate him. I rehearsed the steps I learned in school. Insert ETT and inflate cuff. Done. Good. Attach bag and ventilate. Make sure to listen for sounds in the stomach. Were they listening for sounds in his stomach? What if they missed his trachea and hit his esophagus instead?

"Did you hit his esophagus? Make sure it's not in his

esophagus," I cried out.

One of the EMTs crouched beside me. "He's going to be okay. We've got him intubated."

"What are his vital signs?" I asked.

"They're not very good."

"I want to know what they are."

He looked puzzled.

"I'm a nurse."

"His pulse is slow and weak. He's in v-fib."

They needed to hurry. They weren't moving fast enough. Every second counted. Didn't they know that? Why were they moving so slow? I stood, trying to push my way through the bodies surrounding Noah.

"You've got to get him to the hospital." My entire body shook.

The EMT grabbed my arm and pulled me back.

"Let me go! I want to see him. I know what I'm doing. I want to help." I fought against him but he refused to let go.

"Ma'am, we're taking care of him. We've got him."

Another group of paramedics emerged, carrying the flat board. I'd seen the scene play out so many times before. But this was my kid. My heart. They strapped him to the board. The man didn't let go of me.

"We're going up to the roof. He's going to be airlifted to Children's Hospital," he said.

"Noah! Noah!" My voice changed with every repetition of his name, screeching higher and higher.

"Ma'am, I need you to calm down. Can you tell me your name? I need you to focus on me right now, can you do that?"

My words were swallowed up by my sobs.

He took my head in his hands, fixed his gaze on me. "My name is Carl. I'm going to help you get through this, but I need you to cooperate. What's your name?"

"Adrianne." I didn't recognize my voice.

"Good. That's good. Now, Adrianne, we can have you ride with us to the hospital, but you have to stay calm. I know that's hard, but it's the best thing for Noah right now. I can't let you on the helicopter if you're not calm. Do you understand me?"

I nodded. My body wouldn't stop trembling.

"My people are going to be working with him. He's in the best care. I promise. We're taking care of your boy."

He put his arm around me, and I followed him down the hallway and into the elevator. I heard the sounds of the propellers before we stepped onto the roof. They were loading Noah's body in.

"Here we go," he said.

We covered our heads and ran for the door.

HIM(THEN)

I made it to level three. You get more privileges on level three. I can go to the library as much as I want now and I've filled my room with books. None of the books are new. They're all old classics, things your teacher would assign you to read in school, but I don't care. It's the only time my brain shuts off, and I can disappear for a few hours.

Level three also means they've started talking about my discharge and what happens when I leave. I know it's still a long way off, but just talking about it makes me anxious. Going home scares me. I'm so nervous to see my dad again. He never comes to visit me. It's like he died or something. I'm starting to forget what he looked like and have to work hard to picture his face. Mom doesn't even mention him when she comes. I'm afraid I'll never be able to make things right between us again.

But the thing that scares me the most is losing control of

myself after I'm out. What if it happens again? My counselors all say that I've changed. I'm a mentor to the new kids who come in because I'm supposed to be a model of what a reformed person looks like. They tell my mom that I've made great progress. But have I really changed? Is the darkness still buried somewhere within me? How do I know it's gone? How can I be sure I won't hurt someone again?

13

Noah's heart stopped in the helicopter, and they had to shock him twice before it started again. The doctors put him in a medically induced coma to control the swelling in his brain and hooked him up to a ventilator. I hadn't left his side. I sat in a chair next to his bed and held his hand, listening to the machines beep. Their sounds comforted me because as long as they beeped, I knew he was alive.

I spent hours staring into his face, willing him to open his eyes. The pictures from the balcony flashed through my mind over and over again. They wouldn't stop. It didn't help to look at him in the hospital bed because those images were equally horrific. There was nowhere to look that wasn't filled with pain.

The first twenty-four hours were critical. All the statistics rushed through my head unwanted. How every minute your brain goes without oxygen is damaging. How long had he hung there? Had we found him too late? I knew what it meant if we had. I breathed a sigh of relief when we passed the twenty-four-hour mark without any seizures or signs of cardiac arrest.

The following day his doctors decreased his medicine so that they could check his brain activity. I held my breath and clasped my hands together on my lap while they worked, too scared to move. I burst into tears after his feet responded to stimulation. Over the next two days, they gradually withdrew his medication and slowly woke him up. They removed the tube from his throat when they were confident he could breathe on his own. He opened his eyes, but they weren't focused and moved randomly around the room, sometimes rolling back into his head. He didn't speak and acted as if he didn't hear others who spoke to him. His medical team didn't know how long his brain had gone without oxygen or the extent of his brain damage. Only time would tell.

Time was all I had as I sat in the hospital by myself. I refused to let Lucas visit. I didn't want him anywhere near Noah again. He wouldn't tell me what he said to Noah the night he tried to kill himself, but I knew something he said had pushed him over the edge. Katie begged to visit but children weren't allowed in ICU and even if they were, I wouldn't let her see Noah this way. My mom had been to visit twice, but other than that, I was alone. The window in his room was my only connection to the outside world. I couldn't even bring myself to turn on the TV.

My days were structured by the arrival of nurses and doctors, maintenance workers cleaning up the room, meals, and medications. Some of them asked how I was doing. Others left me alone. I preferred the ones who left me alone. Making small talk was too difficult and it wasn't any easier to talk about Noah's situation. I was stuck in purgatory, unable to think or do anything else except wait for Noah to come back to me.

*****

Even though the nurses assured me that he was in good hands, I couldn't stop myself from speeding on my way back to Dolton. Noah had been out of ICU and in a regular hospital room for three days. He'd finally started to speak but usually just in one-word phrases or answers. They weren't sure if his symptoms were due to neurological damage or depression. They'd added a cocktail of antidepressants to his pain and blood pressure medication. As long as he continued to stabilize, the plan was to move him to the inpatient psychiatric ward by the end of the week. The psychiatric ward was the best place for him. It'd allow him to continue getting all the physical and neurological rehabilitation he needed, but also introduce the psychiatric care that was just as critical to his recovery. The daytime nurses had talked me into going home to get him the things he would need while he was hospitalized. I was grateful that my mom and Lucas had brought my car to the hospital so I didn't have to rent one.

It'd only been two weeks but it felt like years. The world looked different even though nothing had changed. It was like all the sound had been turned off. The colors muted. You couldn't experience the soul-sucking fear of losing your child and come out the same way. You just couldn't.

The apartment was locked, but it didn't matter because the

door was broken from being kicked in. Everything inside was intact and nothing was missing. Maybe it was because we didn't have anything valuable to steal, or people were too afraid to come inside given what happened. The balcony door was ajar. I walked over to shut it and noticed the torn-up sheet lying in pieces where we left it, crumpled up on the balcony. I couldn't bring myself to touch it. Hopefully, the wind would blow it off. I shut the door and pulled the vertical blinds closed so the balcony wouldn't be the first thing Noah saw when he came home.

I threw a few things of mine into a bag. I wanted my own clothes too since I'd been alternating between the clothes I was wearing the night they brought him in and the scrubs the nurses gave me. I didn't need much since they weren't going to let me stay with him once they moved him to the psych ward. I didn't know how I was going to leave him. Not in the condition he was in. But he needed to be safe, and they'd keep him from hurting himself again. No matter how hard it was for me, it was the best thing for him right now. I was waiting for the medication to have an effect. He'd never been on medication before, and I'd always been against antidepressants in kids, but I was willing to try anything that might help because I refused to give up on him even if he was giving up on himself.

I walked into Noah's room to pack his things, unsure of what they'd allow in the psych ward. I'd never been in one before and all the images I'd seen from movies flashed through my mind. I folded his favorite sweatpants and t-shirts in the duffel bag he used for swim meets. I grabbed the book he'd been reading off his nightstand, and that's when it caught my eye—a piece of paper lying on his pillow.

Everyone in the hospital asked if he left a note and I said no, but there it was, beckoning me. I picked it up and took a deep breath, bracing myself for what he thought would be his final words. My hands shook the paper. I wanted to read it, but the lines swerved in front of me, not coming together in coherent sentences. I forced myself to breathe and focus.

Dear Mom,

I love you. This isn't your fault. This is my choice. Tell Katie I love her and will always be her big brother even though I'm gone. Tell Dad he doesn't have to worry about me anymore.

I'm sorry I had to do this to you. If there is a God, I pray you aren't the one to find me. I never wanted to hurt you, Mom. I swear I didn't.

This is best for everyone. I've torn our family apart, and none of you deserve it. You all deserve to have a happy life, and none of you can do that with me in it. I don't want to hurt you or anybody else.

I can't stand the way everyone looks at me. And not because they're wrong. Because they're right. I'm a monster. I know you don't want to believe it, but I am.

I am a pedophile.

You can't treat what I have. It's not ever going to go away. This thing inside of me is who I am and I hate who I am. I can't fix me. Nobody can.

I know who I am. They taught us at Marsh that we weren't pedophiles even though we'd committed a sex crime. They said pedophiles were really rare because it means you're attracted to children. It's disgusting and repulsive, but that's who I'm attracted to. And I know that it's wrong.

I've known this is who I am for years. Ever since seventh grade. I've tried everything I could think of to like girls my own age, but nothing works. I was terrified of ever acting on my attraction because I know it's wrong. Nobody had to teach me that. Nobody had to tell me how much damage I was doing to Maci and Bella by touching them.

I have to live in a world where I can't be around children. Where I can't see them. Where I can't be tempted. But even without any reminders, it's still there. And each time I have the desire, I'm reminded of how sick I am. I don't want to live with this sickness. It won't leave me alone. It doesn't let me sleep. It eats away at me more every day.

I can't hide from it. There's no escaping it. People will always find out. They will always know who I am. They will hate me and attack me like they've always done. And they should. I deserve every hit and broken bone. Next time they might kill me, and I don't blame them. I am going to die, either way.

My mind has never been clearer about what I have to do. Never been sure of anything except this. I have a responsibility to society to make sure I don't hurt anyone else.

I know this will hurt both you and Katie and I'm sorry. Dad will be relieved and Mom, he shouldn't feel bad about that. Please don't hate him when he's glad I'm gone. He's right. He's always seen what you haven't. Please go on to live a happy life. It's all I want for you. It's something I can never have, but you still can. Katie too. Please be sure she does.

And know that I love you. None of this is your fault. Don't take the blame. Nobody could ask for a better mother.

Please don't have a service. Save yourselves the expense. I'd like to be cremated. Burn me and scatter my ashes. Don't keep them. Don't hold on to them. Let me go.

Love,

Noah

I dropped the letter. The light in the room blinded me. I staggered backward. My heartbeat thrashed in my ears. There was a roaring in my head. My thoughts chased each other with lightning speed. His lines repeated. I couldn't breathe. Every wisp of air stolen from my lungs. My intestines churned. I bent over, clutching my gut, trying to stop my body from emptying itself down my legs. My knees were weak. I sank to the floor.

*****

I didn't have any memory of driving to the hospital. One minute I was curled up on Noah's bedroom floor and the next, I was sitting in the parking lot of the hospital with the car running. It had gotten dark. My phone buzzed next to me. I picked it up like I was sleepwalking. My hand looked bigger, like it belonged to someone else.

"Adrianne? Adrianne, are you there?"

I must not have said hello.

"I'm here." My voice reverberated in my head.

"It's Dr. Park. I've been trying to reach you for hours. We were supposed to talk at two. Is everything okay?"

I turned the car off.

"No. It's not. It's not okay." It hurt to talk.

"What happened?"

"He left a note." I barely got the words out before sobs ripped through me. The more I tried to stop crying, the harder the sobs came, each one more intense than the last. She stayed on the line as my anguished cries became silent weeping and waited until the grief had gone beyond tears and sounds to find its way to my center, where it would never leave.

"What'd it say?" she asked.

I swallowed hard and wrestled to gain control of my voice. "He said he was a pedophile." My breath was sharp and shallow.

She was silent, and she was never quiet. She always had something to say.

Finally, she spoke. "It's what I was afraid of."

Afraid? She never said she was afraid.

"What are you talking about?" I asked.

She paused again. The silence stretched out between us. "Are you ready to talk about this? I tried to talk to you about this before. Remember? When he was being discharged?"

"You said you were concerned because he wanted to write the girls a letter. I don't get it. How's that related?"

"I would've been able to explain it to you then if you'd given me a chance, but you didn't want to hear it."

I wasn't sure I wanted to hear it now.

"Noah was an exemplary patient. We've talked about this so many times. He had insight into the ramifications of his actions. He took responsibility. He knew it was wrong. Never denied it. He showed remorse and empathy. There was never a fight on any account. This isn't usually the case. Most kids we work with lack insight into their own behavior. Some of them don't even know it's wrong. They lie more than they tell the truth." She paused, giving me a moment to digest her words. "The only time we don't see this is when we're dealing with kids like Noah, and kids like Noah are rare. Really rare."

"I'm not following you."

"A true pedophile in an adolescent is unusual. It means they have an attraction to children. Most juvenile offenders don't have an attraction to children. The predatory ones are doing it to inflict pain, and children are an easy target because they're vulnerable. There are others who are social misfits and want to have a girlfriend who is their age, but they don't know how or have the skills to do it. So, instead, they experiment with children. Then, there are those who act out because they're under the influence of chemicals or are mentally ill, so they don't know what they're doing. But pedophiles? It's an actual attraction to kids."

As detestable as it was and as much as I didn't want it to be true, her explanation for Noah was the only one that made sense. He didn't fit any of the profiles. Not one. He never had. It always troubled me. The last piece of hope for a better life shattered inside me. There was no grief with it this time. Just an empty hollowness as if the last parts of my insides had been scraped out and discarded. There was nothing left.

"How do you treat them, then?" My voice cracked.

"We don't know how to change the fact that people are sexually attracted to children. The only treatment we can provide is trying to train them how to manage and control their desires."

Her words were a death sentence.

"Being a pedophile doesn't mean they're sexual predators. Sometimes they never touch a child. It doesn't mean he's evil. Nobody has control over who they're attracted to. He can't control who he's attracted to any more than you or I can control our attractions."

Denial was a powerful protective mechanism and I felt naked with mine stripped away.

"We fear what we don't understand, so it's easier to think of them as monsters. It makes us feel safe rather than having to think about the possibility that some people are just born that way, and it could be any of us or someone we love."

"What am I supposed to do?" I asked.

"I wish I knew or had answers to give you, but nobody knows what to do about pedophiles."

14

I stared at the crucifix hanging on the wall in front of me. The altar stood below it with the candles lit. I'd been sitting in the chapel for over an hour, trying to summon up the courage to talk to Noah about his note. He'd been in the psychiatric ward for two days, and I hadn't been able to bring myself to do it.

If anyone would've asked me two years ago if I believed in God, I wouldn't have had to think about my response. It would've been a firm yes, but I didn't know what I believed anymore. What kind of a God would create a person at war with his own body? People hated pedophiles, but nobody hated Noah as much as he hated himself. How could God do that to him?

I went to talk to Father Bob during Noah's pretrial when I was drowning in my depression and afraid I might not make it out. Every day felt like I was walking through mud with concrete slabs tied around my ankles. The priest was usually one of the first people to show up during a crisis, but even Father Bob wouldn't come to see us even though he'd officiated our wedding, christened both our children, and celebrated their confirmation. I was the one who had to go visit him.

My faith was shaken to my core along with everything else. I'd never questioned my faith before because I didn't have a reason to. I'd never doubted God's presence or his goodness. It wasn't as if I was deeply religious. I didn't give much thought to God outside of weekly mass because I believed he was out there working things out for good for the people who lived by his rules, and I'd always lived by his rules as best I could.

I'd expected to meet with Father Bob in his office like we'd done in our other meetings, but he walked me to the back of the church and sat down in the last row of pews. I slid in next to him. I'd never seen him uncomfortable. He couldn't stop shaking his legs and looking over his shoulder like he was afraid someone might catch him with me.

"It's probably best you find another parish," he said before I had a chance to speak.

"Um ... okay, but I'm not sure I want to go to mass anymore. I'm having a hard time with God right now." I tried to hold back my tears. I was working hard at keeping myself together in front of other people. "It's why I came to you. I was hoping you could help."

"You might want to get yourself into counseling."

I nodded. "Counseling is a good idea. I'm sure I'll do some once things with Noah are settled, but I don't know if it's going to help with my feelings toward God. I feel so lost and abandoned. Nothing makes sense. I can't pray or—"

He cut me off. "Sometimes God does things we can't understand."

His answers sounded like they came from a Hallmark card.

"I just—"

He coughed, nervously. "I'm sorry, but I'm really busy right now and need to get back. Take care of yourself." He stood and didn't bother to shake my hand, just left me sitting in the back of the church by myself. He couldn't get away from me fast enough.

I felt as hopeless as I did that day. The door opened and quiet weeping began in the row behind me. I rose, wanting to give the person their sacred space. Besides, I hadn't found any answers here in a long time. I crept out with my head down, trying not to disturb them.

I made my way through the series of hallways that was becoming more and more familiar each passing day. I twisted and turned, winding my way from the east side of the hospital to the west. There wasn't any sign that you were getting close to the psychiatric ward until you came to a series of locked doors. Then, you had to push the call button next to the doors and wait to be buzzed in. Once through, the ward had the same fluorescent lights and pink-tiled hallways as the rest of the hospital. I walked up to the nurse's station and signed myself in on Noah's visitor log. One of the nurses pointed toward the dayroom without looking up.

The dayroom was the place where everyone who wasn't in group therapy or meeting with their psychiatrist congregated. It was also the place where all resemblance to a regular hospital faded away. It looked like the leftovers from a garage sale had been thrown into the room and forgotten. None of the furniture matched. There were beat-up cardboard boxes filled with old magazines and paperback books. Games were scattered all over the tables in the room—jigsaw puzzles with missing pieces, a Scrabble board with missing letters, and a ping-pong table with no paddles. Besides the junk, the room was always filled with people. Some of them sat on the furniture while others manically paced the length of the room. I'd never seen so many people in such a small space with absolutely no interest in interacting with each other. Everyone always seemed like they were in their own world and wanted to be left alone.

I tried not to stare as I walked into the room, because I didn't want to make anyone uncomfortable. I spotted Noah right away. He was sitting in a chair underneath the TV with an unopened magazine in his lap as he stared into space. He was on suicide watch, which meant he had to have a staff member with him at all times. They bothered him with questions about hurting himself every fifteen minutes.

"Is it possible I could talk to him alone in his room?" I asked the woman standing guard beside him like he might try to strangle himself at any moment even though they'd taken away anything he could possibly hurt himself with, including his shoe strings.

"You can't be alone with him in his room, but I can let you into one of the therapy rooms if you'd like," she said.

"That'll work," I said.

We followed her down the hallway on the left and into one of the therapy offices. She opened the door and motioned us inside. The room was small and cramped. It was completely bare. There wasn't even a picture on any of the muted blue walls. There was only a single table with a chair on each side. I sat on one while Noah took the one across from me. It reminded me of the interrogation rooms I'd seen on TV and wasn't anything like Dr. Park's therapy room that was so comfortable and inviting.

"Take all the time you need," she said soothingly, closing the door behind us.

Noah hadn't looked up or spoken, but he rarely spoke

anymore. The doctors weren't sure if it was due to brain damage or what they referred to as catatonic depression. I stared at him like I was seeing him for the first time, trying to imagine what it was like for him and how tortured he must feel. Somehow, I found the strength to break the silence.

"I found your note," I said quietly.

He lifted his head. The first real sign of life in his eyes. "You did?"

I nodded.

"So you know?" His pained stare pierced me.

"Yes, I know." I swallowed the lump in my throat. I opened my mouth, but nothing came out. I didn't have the words for this conversation.

He rubbed his hands down the pale blue scrubs they made every patient wear until they'd earned the privilege of wearing regular clothes. "Did you tell Dad?"

"I didn't tell him." I cleared my throat. Cleared it again. "I'm sorry, Noah. I didn't understand, but I do now, and I still love you."

Tears spilled down my cheeks. I loved him despite what he'd done and who he was.

"Do you?" He cocked his head to the side.

I was taken aback. "Yes, of course I love you. I've always loved you."

"You love who you think I am. Not who I really am." His eyes flared with anger.

"That's not true." His anger took me by surprise.

He jumped up from his chair, pushing it backward as he stood. He slapped his hands on the table in front of us. "Yes, it is,

Mom! I've tried to tell you. Tried to make you see, but you refused. I—"

I stopped him. "You're right. I didn't get it before. But I read your note—"

"So, you get it? You understand I'm a monster? How can you say you love me, then? I'm a fuckin' monster." He grabbed his chair and threw it against the wall. The nurse from the hallway rushed in.

"What's going on?" Her eyes never moved past Noah. She cautiously stepped toward him.

"It's okay. We're okay. He just got upset for a moment. We're fine." I motioned for the door. "You can go. Really, we're okay."

Noah paced the room, frantically rubbing his hands up and down his arms so hard I was afraid he'd rub himself raw. She didn't look convinced.

"If I need you, I'll call you," I said, motioning to the door again.

She backed away cautiously. This time, she left the door open a crack.

"Noah, please sit down," I pled in the same voice I used to use when he was a toddler and I had to coax him down from the top of a piece of furniture he'd climbed on.

He shook his head, breathing in and out rapidly. "Don't you get it? Can't you see? I deserve to be dead. People like me shouldn't be allowed to live." His face was contorted in agony as if someone was physically hurting him.

I got up and took a step toward him. "I get it," I said quietly, keeping my voice even and calm. "Please hear me when I say I love you, and I understand."

He leaned over and let out a cry of grief so raw I felt it in my body. I rushed to his side, taking him in my arms like I'd done so many times in the past. But unlike all the times before, I didn't tell him that it was going to be okay because it wasn't. He'd always known that. I held him in my arms while he came apart and sobs ripped through him. I refused to let go as his wailing moved from violent waves to soft whimpering, to jerking breaths of nothing after he was finally spent. I guided him back to his chair and delicately sat him in it. I moved my chair around the table to sit next to him.

He turned to me with tears and snot running down his face. "I want to die." His eyes were tortured, haunted with images I couldn't imagine. All the pictures of what he'd done, what he was afraid of doing, and what had been done to him.

I took his hand in mine. I was out of words to say and done trying to pretend I had any answers.

"I'm going to do it again. You can't stop me," he said.

Was he talking about killing himself or hurting kids? Did it matter?

*****

I made the two-hour drive to the hospital for visiting hours every day. Some days we talked. Others we just sat in silence. Today Lucas had brought Katie to visit. He'd dropped her off in the waiting room and then left, making up some excuse for not being able to stay. It was the first time she'd seen him since he went into the hospital. Children weren't allowed in ICU and I hadn't let her visit even after he was transferred to a regular room because I didn't want her to see him in his catatonic state. It would've frightened her too much. The bruises around his neck were fading but still visible so I'd brought him a white turtleneck to wear underneath his hospital scrubs. We hadn't told Katie exactly what he'd done, only that he'd tried to hurt himself and had to be in the hospital until the doctors were sure he wouldn't try to hurt himself again.

They spent the visit playing Uno quietly and coloring in one of her favorite coloring books. She kissed him on the cheek softly when the visit was over and promised to be back soon. Her strength and fortitude moved me as I watched her struggle to keep her tears inside and be strong for him as she left.

"When did you know?" I asked after she was gone.

"Huh? What do you mean?"

"That you ... that you, um ..."

"That I was sick?"

I nodded.

"In seventh grade."

He said that in his note. It was folded in my purse and I carried it with me every day. I hadn't worked up the nerve to read it again. I wasn't sure I ever would.

"You just all of a sudden knew?"

"Not really. Not like that."

"So, then what happened?"

He raised his eyebrows at me. "Are you really sure you want to know?"

I nodded, steeling myself for what he was about to disclose.

He took a deep breath. "Well, it was when all my friends started getting into girls. Kyle was obsessed and figured out all the parental controls on his computer so he could start looking at porn. We used to watch it together." He turned bright red and looked away. "Sorry, Mom."

I wanted to laugh. I wished his problem was watching porn.

"He'd get so excited, and I didn't see what the big deal was. Everyone else was the same way. It was like overnight everyone got girl crazy, and I didn't. Honestly, for a while, I thought I might be gay. God, I wish I was gay ..."

I did too.

He stared into space, wrestling with his demons. I waited for him to continue.

"But then, I started having all these weird thoughts on the bus. I'd be sitting in the back and find myself staring at the elementary girls as they got on. I couldn't stop staring or thinking about them. I was obsessed. None of it was sexual at first. I don't know how to explain it, but I wanted to be their friends. They looked so precious and adorable."

He looked at me, studying my reaction. I willed my face to remain expressionless and open to what he had to say even though part of me wanted to tell him to stop talking. I wasn't sure I wanted to know what came next. I forced myself to remain calm. I'd spent months trying to get him to talk to me. He finally was, and I had to be open to what he had to say no matter how horrific it might be. I nodded at him, signaling him to continue.

"It was weird, and I knew it. I was like, what the hell is wrong with me? I'd never paid attention to them before, barely noticed they were on our bus. But all of a sudden, I was so aware of them. I noticed them everywhere I went. And then there was this one little girl who sat alone on the bus every day. She was so cute, but she didn't have any friends who sat with her. I started fantasizing about her. At first, it was just about being her friend, kinda like her big brother. I thought about going to sit with her in her seat and talking to her about her day. Is this making you sick?"

I shook my head, hoping he couldn't tell I was lying.

"I know when the kids at Marsh used to tell their stories, I'd get sick hearing them. I used to throw up in the bathroom after group sessions."

"I'm fine," I assured him even though I wasn't.

"Then, it started to get sexual. Not bad, though, Mom. I swear I never actually wanted to hurt a kid. I just wanted to hug and cuddle with her. But thinking about touching her aroused me. That's when I knew something was seriously wrong with me. Before it seemed really weird, but once it crossed over that line, I knew it was sick—that I was sick. I'm still sick. I'm sorry. I'm so sorry."

He wasn't looking at me. I wasn't sure who he was apologizing to—himself, the girls, me, the world.

"That was in seventh grade?"

He nodded.

But it was two years until he acted out. At least that's what he said. Did he hurt other girls? Were there other things we didn't know about?

"I swore I'd never touch a little girl and decided I'd kill myself if I did. I focused on school and swimming. I put all my energy into it. Every night, I prayed for God to take it away. Sometimes I thought it worked because I'd go for a few months and wouldn't have any thoughts. No urges. I thought maybe he'd answered my prayer. But then something would happen, and I'd be hit with it all over again. I tried everything, Mom. I did. I tried thinking about Katie. How I'd feel if someone did something like that to her. Tried pretending they were Katie, because I swear to God, Mom, I was never attracted to Katie."

At least I was right about something.

"And then, that summer, that awful summer ... I should've known it was a bad idea to coach the pee-wee league. I don't know what I was thinking." He shook his head quickly. "That's not true. I do know what I was thinking—I didn't think I was capable of touching a little girl. I knew it was wrong, and it went against every part of me. I know that doesn't make sense. But then, we'd be in the pool, and you'd have to hold them and help them. Sometimes they'd rest on my leg. And I got aroused ..." His face turned bright red. For the first time since he'd started talking, he looked away. "I had no control of it. My body just did it. I was trapped. I couldn't jump out of the pool because then everyone would see. I didn't know what to do, and then Maci touched it. She touched it and asked what it was."

I gripped my chair, afraid I'd fall on the floor if I let go. My entire body swayed.

"It was so innocent. So sweet." His face was contorted in confusion. Torn even now.

"I know what happened next." I couldn't take it anymore. I heard the full confession of the touching in court. I barely made it through that time. I couldn't hear it again. Not from his mouth. It was bad enough when they read it as a formal statement.

"I told myself I'd kill myself if I ever acted on it and fully intended to do it. I'd lay in my room for hours trying to work up the nerve. Killing myself was all I thought about, but I was so scared. Scared I'd burn in hell. Scared to hurt you and Dad. Katie. Then, I started thinking about what would happen if I told someone. I wasn't thinking about telling someone to get help. I was thinking about prison. I wanted someone to lock me up so I couldn't hurt anyone. That's when I came to you."

That night. The one that changed everything.

"I didn't want to go to Marsh, but everyone said it would help me, so I went. And then once I was there, I started getting hopeful because Dr. Park said all we had to do was follow their program, and we'd be better. She promised. I did everything, Mom. Every single thing. I wanted to be better so bad. More than I've ever wanted anything. I tried so hard, but it didn't go away. None of it. And then when Rick came to visit and showed me the pictures of his new girlfriend, I knew I was hopeless. That guy was such a loser, Mom, but he'd gotten better. He'd changed and I was never going to. It didn't matter how hard I tried."

"Is that why you took the pills?"

He nodded.

"What'd your dad say to you the night you ..." My question trailed off.

"Have you asked him about it?"

I shook my head. "We're not talking."

He'd been to visit Noah in the hospital twice, and I hadn't spoken a word to him. I left as soon as he arrived and didn't come back until he was ready to go. I didn't give him updates on Noah. If he cared, then he could check with the medical staff himself.

"I know you're pissed at Dad, but you shouldn't be."

"Let me worry about your dad," I said.

He shrugged his shoulders.

"I still want to know what he said." I had to find out what pushed him over the edge. Swallowing pills was emotional and impulsive, but hanging himself took thought, planning, and preparation. He had plenty of time to think about what he was doing and change his mind, but he didn't.

"You're going to get pissed off."

"Believe me, I'm already pissed at your dad. I want to know what happened."

"If I tell you, then you have to promise not to tell him I told you."

Lucas and I didn't keep secrets. Never had, especially when it came to our kids, but we weren't who we used to be.

"I won't tell him," I said.

"He said I should run away. He told me to leave a note for you and Katie and tell you I was leaving. He promised to pay for my plane ticket to California no matter what it cost and drive me to the airport. I have no idea why he chose California. I guess because it's as far west as you can get without leaving the country. Anyway, he said he'd send me money every month. The only catch was that I couldn't contact you or anyone in the family ever again. He swore he'd cut me off if I did. He promised to send me money until I was twenty-one and after that I'd be on my own."

My stomach churned. Vehement anger shot through my veins. How could he do something like that? How could he exile him away without talking to me about it? What did he think Noah would do after hearing something like that?

"I'm sorry he put you in that position. No wonder you tried to kill yourself."

Noah shook his head. "No, he was right. That's not why I tried to kill myself. I thought about he suggested and I agreed with him. It actually made perfect sense. I'd wrecked all your lives, and it was never going to get easier. You were going to give up your entire life to take care of me and Katie would lose out. She's already missed out on so much. She'd never get to have a normal life, and she deserves a normal life. You and Dad were going to split up eventually. I know you try to pretend like it's not my fault, but you guys would be happy if it wasn't for me."

"That's—"

He raised his hand. "Mom, stop. You don't need to keep trying to protect me. I'm okay with the truth. Let's just tell the truth. Okay, please?"

I hung my head.

"It was the one thing I could do to make things better. But, I was afraid of what I'd do out there on my own. Not that I wouldn't be able to make it. I would've found some way to support myself, but I was terrified of touching a girl again. I swore before that I'd never act on my urges, but then I did, and I couldn't stop, so how could I trust myself? I can never do what I did again. Ever."

I grabbed his hands, gripping them both in mine, and peered over the table at him. Our noses almost touched. "So, then you won't. You never have to do that again." I drew each word out, stressing *never*.

He pulled his hands away, moving back in his chair. "I can't say I won't do something again. I just can't. I don't know for sure."

I shook my head with fiery determination, refusing to accept his truth. "It's possible. People refuse to act on their urges all the time. Look at drug addicts. They're faced with temptation every day and choose not to act on it."

"It's not that simple. There's so much more to it than that. I hate myself. Every part of me, even the parts that used to be good. I meant what I said in my letter. I was doing what was best for everyone in the situation and if you think about it, Mom, it really is."

I shook my head. I wouldn't hear of it.

"You can't stop me. I'm going to do it again." His eyes were set with determination. This time, there was no mistaking what he was talking about.

"Noah, no. Please, stop. Don't talk like that." An image of him hanging from the balcony flashed through my mind. I squeezed my eyes shut tightly, trying to make the picture disappear. "You're doing so much better than you were."

The team of psychiatrists and doctors responsible for his care had been giving me positive reports. They were pleased and optimistic that he'd turned around and begun to take steps toward his healing. He was participating in group, something he hadn't done up until this point, and responsive in his therapy sessions whereas before he sat curled up in a ball in his chair, staring, and mumbling his answers. At times, he was incoherent. They attributed his turnaround to the antidepressants finally taking an effect. They were hopeful he'd continue to make gains.

His eyes flashed with anger. "Do you know why I'm doing better?" He put air quotes on "doing better." "I want out of here, and that's not going to happen unless they think I'm not suicidal. I'm not an idiot."

One of the staff members peeked her head into the room. She was the dark-haired nurse who worked most days. I was beginning to recognize all of them.

"Sorry, visiting hours are up," she said with a smile I'd never seen her without. I didn't know how she stayed so cheerful in a place like this.

I couldn't leave. Not now. Not after everything he'd shared. What if he did something tonight? I furtively looked around his room, searching for anything he might hurt himself with. There was nothing. I breathed a sigh of relief. He was safe as long as he was in the hospital. I just had to find a way to keep him there.

15

"Thanks for taking the time to meet with me," I said as I took a seat in Dr. Phillips office. It was the first time I'd been in her office. Most of our conversations were on the phone or standing in the hallway outside of Noah's room. Her office was cramped with a large oak desk that was too big for the space. Bookshelves lined the walls overflowing with self-help titles like *Healing Your Emotional Self* and *The Anxiety Workbook for Teens.*

"I'm sorry it's such a mess. I usually don't hold meetings in here." She'd agreed to squeeze me in on her lunch break and took a bite of her Subway sandwich. "What's going on?"

I didn't want to waste any time. "I'm worried about Noah. I'm afraid he's going to kill himself when he gets out."

She wiped her face with a napkin. "That's a totally normal reaction. Every parent who's been through what you've been through would feel the same way. It's a terrifying experience to almost lose your child."

"Yes, it is, but that's not what I'm talking about." I hesitated for a minute. I didn't want to betray his confidence, but what choice did I have? "He told me he's going to try to kill himself again when he gets out. He's only pretending to be better so you let him out."

She set her sandwich on the desk, taking a drink of her soda. "He said those exact words?"

"Basically." I wrung my hands together on my lap.

"I'm surprised by that. Today in group he agreed to attend a support group for teenagers who've tried to commit suicide. He told me in our session yesterday that he wants to start having Skype sessions with the psychologist he worked with at Marsh to process some of the struggles he's still having with his sexual urges. All of that is very significant."

"He's only saying it so you'll let him out." My voice rose. "You have to keep him in the hospital. You can't discharge him. You just can't. He's not ready."

"We're not saying he's ready, but he's taking steps in the right direction. We can't keep people in the hospital who are no longer a threat to themselves."

"But he is! Even if he says he isn't, he is!" I could no longer keep the hysteria out of my voice.

"Have you thought about getting some help for yourself? Someone you can talk to about your fears?"

"They're not fears." I bit my cheek to keep from crying.

Her eyes filled with compassion. "There's nothing more terrifying than almost losing your child."

"If you let him out and he kills himself, I'll sue the hospital." I'd never threatened another person. It felt strange but I'd do anything to keep him safe.

"Listen, Adrianne." She rolled up her sandwich and stuffed it back in the bag. "Nobody wants to release your son if he's a threat to himself. We're going to do everything we can to make sure he isn't discharged until we've given him the best possible psychiatric care and he's no longer a danger to himself or anyone else. That's the role of an inpatient hospital. It doesn't mean his work is done once we release him. It's just that we want to treat him in the least restrictive environment, and the hospital is the most restrictive. We're not going to stop treating him after he's discharged. We'll just treat him on an outpatient basis. Has anyone explained our outpatient program to you?"

I shook my head.

"He's a great candidate for successful outpatient treatment. He'll still come to the hospital every day and participate in all of the groups and therapy. It will be exactly the same except he won't be sleeping here."

It wasn't good enough. If he was out, he'd have the opportunity.

"He has to stay in the hospital."

Dr. Phillips came to sit next to me. She placed her hand tentatively on my knee. "I hear what you're saying, and I take your concerns seriously. I'm going to share them with the rest of his care team. I'll make sure to take extra time with him during our sessions to assess if he's still acutely suicidal. He's not going to be discharged in the next couple days, so why don't you take some time to take care of yourself? Get some rest. You must be exhausted."

She had no idea. I'd never been so tired. I wanted to crawl into bed and sleep for months. But each time I tried to sleep, my body wouldn't allow it. My mind raced. I hadn't been sleeping for more than a few hours. My sleeping pills had no effect. All they did was make me feel foggier than I already was. I didn't know if I'd ever be rested again, but how could I sleep when my son's life teetered on the edge of death?

*****

Each time they gave me a positive report on Noah, the threat of impending doom increased. It followed me everywhere I went. Dr. Phillips assured me she was thorough in her questions about his mental state. She gave him a host of psychological tests that showed he was no longer suicidal; even his depression scores decreased. More and more our conversations centered on preparing for his treatment once he was out, but I didn't care what their tests said. He needed to stay in the hospital. It was the only place he was safe.

"I know you're scared, Mom," Noah said as we played our latest card game, Phase 10. We'd grown tired of Uno and let Katie pick out a new one on her last visit.

"What do you mean?" I shifted in my seat.

"I know you're totally freaked out about ... well, you know ... what we talked about before." He looked over his shoulder at the door to his room.

It'd been six days since he told me he planned on ending his life when he got out. He hadn't brought it up since.

"Are you still thinking about it?"

"People with terminal illnesses do it all the time," he said.

"But you don't have a terminal illness."

"I suffer from a condition that doesn't have a cure. What's the difference?"

He may only have been seventeen but he was no longer a child. He was logical, rational, and smart.

"You have things to live for." It sounded so clichéd but I had to say it.

"Like?" He cocked his head to the side.

"Katie. Think about how much she loves you. Can you imagine how devastated she'll be to lose her brother? You're her hero. Always have been." It was the first thing that came to me.

He shook his head. "There will come a day when she hates me. She's too young to understand now, but believe me, once she's older and finds out what I did and who I am, it'll change how she feels about me. Her perception. Who I am to her. All of it. She's not going to want me around."

Was what he said true? How would she feel about him when she was older? Was there any way to know?

"What about me?" It was selfish to ask him to consider staying alive so I wouldn't have to go through the pain of losing him, but I couldn't help myself.

"I'd be giving you a gift—you'd get your life back." He said it with so much tenderness it made me want to weep. "You could help me ..."

"What are you talking about?"

"You could be there with me this time. Make sure I didn't wake up." He said it in such a way that I could tell it wasn't the first time he'd thought about it. His plans hadn't gone anywhere.

I ferociously shook my head. "No way. Absolutely not."

"What if I was dying of cancer? Would you help me die if I had cancer and was only going to suffer by being alive?"

"That's entirely different. You don't have cancer."

He gave me a halfhearted smile. "You're right. I've got something worse. At least when you have cancer people still love you."

HIM(THEN)

I am finally learning how to retrain my brain. I didn't think it would ever happen for me, but it is. I made it through the entire round of pictures without a reaction. They even showed me the one with the little girl on the swing. Nothing. I'm so happy I could cry.

I've discovered other tricks too. Whenever my mind starts to wander to places it shouldn't, I pinch my thigh really hard. I have dark purple bruises on the insides of both legs but I don't care. It's working. It stops the thoughts, and I'll do anything to stop the thoughts.

It helps that I don't have to keep talking about what I did over and over again anymore. Most of the talk in group focuses on how I'll handle temptation once I'm out. I know one thing for sure—I'm not going anywhere near little girls. Ever. I won't even put myself in that situation.

I'm going keep to myself. I'll focus on my schoolwork and nothing else. Maybe if I try really hard I can graduate early. I'm not going to talk to anyone at school. I'm going to do my best to make myself invisible just like I've done here. I've gotten really good at it. Sometimes I feel like I'm just a ghost.

I want to go to college early. I don't know how my mom will feel about that but I want to get as far away from home as possible. I can't start over there, and all I want is a new start. I want to put this behind me. Bury it somewhere so I never have to think about it again.

If only I never had to sleep. I can't control my thoughts in my sleep. My dreams take on a life of their own and sometimes they move into old behavior. I dream about what it felt like. How much I liked it. I told my counselor about the dreams. She says it's normal and just my unconscious working things out, but I didn't tell her what I'm doing to myself when I wake up. That part is too embarrassing.

16

I spent each visit trying to help Noah find reasons to stay alive. It was like he was standing on a ledge getting ready to jump and I was the person who found him there. I reminded him of things that made him feel happy and tried to convince him that he was still valuable. I rehearsed what I would say on the drive, trying to come up with things I hadn't thought of before.

I grappled with recording our conversations and sharing them with Dr. Phillips. It would be easy to do. All I'd have to do was wear my baggy linen pants with the deep pockets, put my phone in one of them, and press record. She'd have no choice but to keep him in the hospital, but he'd never trust me again if I did that. Besides, there would come a time he had to leave even if I convinced them to keep him longer. I'd finally accepted that he couldn't stay forever and if I betrayed him, he'd stop talking to me and I'd lose any possibility of helping him. At least if I knew what he was planning, then I could stop him.

He'd started looking at me again when he talked. For so long, his eyes had stared through me or past me, but never at me. Now, he really looked because, for the first time since he confessed, I finally saw him and understood. He was my son, and he was also a pedophile. I accepted his truth, but just because I accepted it didn't mean he needed to die because of it.

"What if they find a way to cure it within the next ten years? Like they can give you a drug to take every day, and it wipes it all out?" I asked.

"Do you honestly think anyone is going to spend money trying to fix us? Taking hard-earned cash and spending the resources to fix people they hate? Who's going to fund the research? And how are they going to test it? Send a bunch of pedophiles to a playground and see what happens?" He snorted. "Besides, they've already found out a way to chemically castrate people, and that hasn't helped."

"Really?"

"Yep, I looked it up."

I did the same when I got home, and he was right. Although many of the drugs decreased libido and the number of urges, their primary effect was on increasing impulse control and helping them resist acting out. Doctors described the drugs as turning down the volume on the radio. They may have found a way to turn down the volume, but nobody knew how to turn it off.

I shifted my focus the next day. "Can't you find a way to make some kind of meaning out of your suffering? Form a group to help others? Write a book?"

He laughed and rolled his eyes at me. "What kind of help would I offer people? Hey, don't worry, you're not alone. I like kids too. Then what? We sit around and drink coffee talking about the fact that we'll never be better? The point of support groups is to help people get better."

When I had nothing left, I pulled things out of the sky. "What if you have the cure to cancer, and you don't know it yet? You could save so many lives."

"That's about as likely as me figuring out a way to get to the moon."

I was running out of solutions that didn't include losing him forever.

He locked his eyes with mine. "I'll spend every day that I'm alive hating myself. Tell me the truth—if it was you, would you want to live that way?"

I wanted to lie and say I would if it meant he'd stay, but I couldn't bring myself to do that to him. I swallowed the tears in my throat and whispered, "I don't know."

"You still haven't answered my question."

I raised my eyebrows. "What are you talking about?"

"If I had cancer and was going to die a slow painful death, would you respect my choice to end my life?"

I shook my head. "We've already had this conversation. It's not the same thing, not even close. You don't have cancer. You're not going to die from it."

"Really? How long before someone beats the shit out of me again? You think that was the last time?" He paused before whispering as an afterthought, "You don't even know what they did to me."

"What did you say?" I asked.

"Nothing," he mumbled, looking away. "Forget about it."

I stood, putting my hands on my hips. "What did you say,

Noah?"

He glanced at the door. "Mom, please, I don't want to talk about it."

"I heard you—you said that I didn't even know what they did to you. What did you mean?"

He gulped. "You can't tell anyone. No one. Not even Dr. Park." His body tightened, and he worked his jaw as he spoke. "If you tell anyone, I'll deny it. I'll swear you made it up."

Fear rose in my throat.

He got up and shut the door, a privilege he was allowed since he was no longer on suicide watch and could be trusted alone in his room. It seemed like he was moving in slow motion as he took a seat on his bed. He pulled his legs up to his chest, clutching them with his arms.

"They didn't just use the bat to beat me." His eyes stared through me.

My head swirled, threatening to roll off my neck. The walls were breathing—inhaling and exhaling around me. "What—but I ... you didn't ... how–I–wh-wh ... you mean, they, they ..."

"Raped me." The color drained from his face.

All the energy got sucked out of the room. My heart pounded in my temples. The room spun quickly before it stilled again, leaving me nauseous. I sifted through the snapshots of that day. So much blood on his jeans. The way he walked—crooked, hunched over, gripping his stomach. The ride to the hospital. Curled up on his side. The signs were there. I hadn't looked. Never imagined. It never entered my awareness. It seemed like an eternity passed before I spoke again.

"Why didn't the doctors tell me?" I asked.

"They didn't know." His voice was flat, devoid of emotion.

That was impossible.

"How could they not have known?"

"They used the skinny part of the bat," he explained as if that made any sense. "You packed me clothes, remember?"

Somehow, I had the presence of mind to throw together some things for him before we left for the hospital that day. I nodded, signaling that I remembered.

"I stuffed my underwear with toilet paper when I was changing into my gown. I never told anyone."

"God, no, Noah—"

I jumped up, clasping my hand over my mouth, flung open his door, and raced down the hallway to the bathroom. My stomach heaved into my hand, forcing what was already in it to spray through my fingers. I rushed to the stall, kneeling before the toilet, and emptied what was left in my mouth into the toilet bowl. Wave after wave of nausea racked my body. I heaved until there wasn't anything left but green and yellow mucus snaking its way down the toilet.

My head pounded when I stood, and I steadied myself against the bathroom stall. My eyes burned, and my throat was raw. I put my mouth under the faucet and washed it out. I splashed water on my face, refusing to look at myself in the mirror. How could they? How could anyone do that to my son? I wanted to curl up in a ball on the floor and sob. I forced myself to move and plodded back to Noah's room. He hadn't moved from his position on the bed.

"Honey, I'm so sorry." I reached for him.

He pulled back. "Don't, Mom. Just don't. I'm not telling you so you feel sorry for me. I'm telling you so that you'll understand."

"How can people do that? How can they be so cruel?" Just when I thought my heart couldn't break any more, the last pieces of it shattered.

"It's what people do to child molesters. Everyone cheers when they get sent to prison because they know what's going to happen. Do you think anyone cares? Tries to stop it? No, because nobody cares. I want to die with dignity, Mom. It's what it's called–dying with dignity—and I may not deserve anything else, but I deserve that."

"You really call swinging from our balcony dying with dignity?" The question flew out of my mouth without thinking.

"Then help me, Mom. Please, help me." His eyes begged for understanding, pleading with me. "Please."

It was at that moment that I decided I would.

17

I lay curled up next to Katie watching her sleep. I was a stranger in my own house. I'd been gone for so long I could smell the house in the same way you smelled other people's homes when you entered them. I smelled it because it was no longer mine. It was theirs.

I hadn't spent any quality time with Katie in over two weeks. I'd seen her during her visits at the hospital but hadn't spent any time with her alone. Noah encouraged me to spend the night with her because he noticed subtle changes coming over her. There was a new heaviness in the way she held herself, and a cloud of sadness passed through her eyes when she didn't think anyone was looking.

Lucas was worried about her too. He pulled me aside after dinner and told me to make sure I put a towel underneath her when she went to sleep because she'd started to wet the bed again. She refused to wear pull-ups, said they were for babies. She hadn't wet the bed since she was four.

I tried to focus and give her all my attention while we played with her new Barbie house and read the latest Harry Potter book before bed, but I couldn't get the images of Noah being sexually assaulted to stop playing. It'd been that way for three days. I couldn't think of anything else. They pummeled into my consciousness no matter what I was doing. I would be sitting in front of my computer trying to lose myself in work when suddenly I was confronted with the image of a bloody bat or the way his face looked the day he told me about his attack. I wasn't sure I'd ever forget the look of anguish and utter demoralization in his eyes.

How many times had I heard "I hope he gets raped in jail" during his trial or seen it written in black Sharpie ink on the flyers posted around town? Or in the stream of comments underneath every article written about him online? It tortured me to think about the pain he must've endured in silence. Not only the emotional pain, but he had to be in excruciating physical pain too, and he never said anything. I'd heard all the stories about people getting raped in prison because child molesters were treated as the worst kind of criminals, even behind bars. Rape was wrong unless you were raping a child molester. We forgave murderers, not pedophiles.

The boys who raped him were the real monsters. How sick did a kid have to be to assault someone with a bat and leave them to die? And he could've died that day. They left him beaten, bloody, and unconscious. And yet, they were likely sitting at home preparing for final exams or getting ready for their next big game. The police did nothing to find or punish them as soon as they found out who Noah was. Their job was to serve and protect, but those rules didn't apply to Noah.

All he did was touch the girls. There was no penetration or

insertion of any kind. Each of them had been taken to the pediatrician for an examination, and neither showed signs of sexual assault, because he hadn't assaulted them. He'd touched them, and they'd touched him. That's all. It didn't make it right. It was disgusting and wrong, but he didn't physically hurt them. Not even close to how he'd been brutalized and stripped of his dignity.

If he'd been their age, it would've been labeled innocent fun. Playing doctor. It wasn't as if he'd forced himself on them. He hadn't. They'd been the ones to touch first. I didn't blame the girls, though. It wasn't their fault. They had no idea what they were doing. None. Their touch and exploration was completely innocent. Nothing sexual about it, but it hadn't been innocent for Noah, and he wasn't their age, which made it a crime. I understood that, but their lives weren't going to be ruined forever. They just weren't. But, the world wouldn't be satisfied until they'd annihilated him. He was more of a victim than those girls, but society would never see it that way. They saw it as him getting what he deserved.

I hadn't slept since he told me. Not one hour. Tonight was no different. I wanted to cry, but couldn't anymore. I'd been drained of my tears, hollowed out, and a cold numbness had settled over me, leaving me cut off from the rest of the world. In the most private part of myself, I considered doing it together. I pictured us lying side by side on his bed as we drifted toward our death. The images flashed when I didn't want them to. I tried to push them away, but they refused to be ignored.

I was exhausted. Every shred of fight had dwindled down to nothing. I felt like a shell of a person and couldn't remember what it felt like to really be alive. Yet, no matter how awful I felt, it didn't compare to the pain Noah was going through. No wonder he wanted to die.

I spent my sleepless nights scouring the Internet and gathering information on the Death with Dignity Act. At first, I felt like I was going to throw up because helping someone die went against everything I'd been taught. I approached it like I'd done my first year of nursing school, when I overcame fainting at the sight of blood. The fainting episodes almost derailed my dream because no one wants a nurse who ends up on the floor every time they stick a needle in your arm. I started chanting, "I'm not going to faint," each time I pulled out a needle and rehearsed it silently until the feelings of lightheadedness passed. I changed my mantra to "I'm not going to throw up" until I could read the research without the reaction.

The Death with Dignity Act was based on the premise that we chose how to live our lives and should be able to choose how we wanted to die. Proponents claimed it was a basic right to control when and how you died. It brought up so many questions I'd never thought about. Should people be forced to live when they didn't want to? Why was I fighting so hard for Noah to stay alive when he so clearly wanted to die? Was it fair to ask him to stay alive so I didn't have to live without him?

If he was dead, he'd never know if his sexual response system would've changed, but as much as I wanted change to be a possibility, I'd always liked boys. My attraction hadn't veered since I was a nine-year-old girl and had my first crush on Billy Corgin. I still remembered the smell of his green apple bubble gum he snapped all through fourth grade. Nothing was going to change Noah's attraction either. He couldn't change his physiological response any more than I could change mine.

He was going to live in continual torture—isolated, stigmatized, and alone. How would it be to live his entire life repressing something that was perfectly normal for most people? How could I ever keep him out of situations where he might be blamed? He'd always look guilty even if he was innocent, and there wasn't any way to keep people from finding out about him. He was registered, and all you had to do was google his name to find it. His Facebook page was still there despite my continued contacts to Facebook to take it down. There wasn't any way to protect him when others found out. Never had been. How many more times would he be beaten and raped?

Everything on death with dignity was related to people with terminal illnesses. I was fascinated with their stories and devoured them. I read and watched everything on Brittany Maynard. I hadn't paid much attention to her case when it happened, but I couldn't tear myself away from it. She was only twenty-nine when she was diagnosed with a horrible form of brain cancer and given six months to live. Treatments would only diminish her quality of life, and she wanted to enjoy her last moments. But most importantly, she didn't want to put herself or her family through watching her deteriorate to a point where she was unrecognizable. She and her husband moved to Oregon where it was legal. She spoke so eloquently about her choice to save herself and others from needless suffering. As I scrolled through page after page of her experience and others like her, I had to ask myself the same question Noah asked me: would I help him die if he had terminal cancer? The truth—no matter how much I didn't want to admit it—was that if Noah was dying of brain cancer and didn't want to suffer, I would help end his suffering. Was his condition any less vile, debilitating and dignity-robbing than brain cancer?

I would go to jail if anyone found out I helped him. Could I risk not being there for Katie in order to help Noah? Was that fair to her? I could never tell her that I helped her brother die. She'd hate me for it. There was no question about that. I'd have to lie to her for the rest of her life. Could I live with a secret that huge? Was I prepared to live with what I'd done for the rest of my life?

Lucas's reaction was the only one I didn't have to worry about. He'd be happy Noah was gone. I blamed him for so much of Noah's hopelessness and despair. His rejection was as painful as any fist. I couldn't shake the feeling that he was the one who finally pushed him over the edge and put the gun in his hand. I couldn't wrap my brain around him telling him to leave and disappear from our family forever. In a sense, I was doing the same thing, but I was doing it because I loved him and didn't want him to continue to suffer, and I never would've considered it if he hadn't been the one to ask. Lucas wanted to get rid of him because he hated him. Period. I didn't care if our actions might be similar, our intentions were entirely different.

I hadn't told Noah that I'd decided to help him. There would be no going back once I told him. It would set a plan in motion and make it a reality. I kept waiting to be ready to tell him what I'd decided, but I was never going to be ready. I just had to do it.

*****

The drive to the hospital the next day was similar to how I felt when I was in labor. The moments leading up to it were so surreal because the life you knew was about to be changed forever and never going to look the same. Today was no different. Each mile brought me closer to the inevitable consequences of agreeing to help Noah.

He was sitting in the community room watching an old movie with some of the other patients when I got there. He jumped up to greet me as soon as he saw me in the doorway and led the way down the hallway to his room. He didn't have to ask permission to go to his room anymore. All his restrictions had been lifted because nobody worried about his safety. They were convinced he was on the road to recovery.

He plopped down on his bed and crossed his legs. "How'd it go with Katie? Did you give her the picture I made for her?"

I nodded. Lately, they'd been working on a comic book together. Each one worked on a page that they traded once they'd finished and then the other continued the story where it left off. Noah had never been the creative type, her illustrations far better than his, but they both loved it, and it kept them connected. I promised her we'd find a way to put it together in a real comic book with binding and laminated pages once it was finished.

"All of this is starting to have an effect on her," I said, sadness thickening my voice.

His eyes filled with concern. "What's going on?"

"She's started to wet the bed at night. Your dad also said her teachers have been saying she seems like she's having a harder time concentrating."

"Poor Peanut. This has got to be so tough on her. I'm surprised she's lasted this long."

It was only a matter of time until she started suffering from everything going on. I needed to get her into therapy and give her a place to talk about things without having to worry about my feelings. It was hard to imagine my gentle and imaginative seven-year-old needing therapy. None of this was anything like the life I imagined. It was all wrong.

"I'm going to talk to your dad about getting her some help." I paused, searching for the strength to go on. "And I want to talk to you about something too ..."

He nodded, waiting for me to continue.

"I've been thinking about what you asked me."

His eyes lit up. He knew exactly what I was referring to. It was the question that had hung in the air expectantly since he posed it.

"Do you still feel the same way?" I asked.

He didn't have to take time to think about his answer. "Absolutely."

I took a deep breath, whispering a silent prayer of forgiveness. "I've decided I'm going to help you."

His eyes widened. "Are you serious? Really? Are you serious?"

I nodded, pushing past the lump in my throat. "If you're convinced this is what you want to do, then I'll make sure it's easy for you. I don't want you to have to do something awful to yourself again, and I don't want you to be alone during it."

My words sent shockwaves through my body.

A wide grin spread across his face. He clasped his hands together. "Thank you, Mom. Thank you so much." He stood to come toward me.

I motioned for him to sit down. "Don't. Not yet."

The enormity of what I'd agreed to filled the whole room. It was hard to breathe. My entire world felt like it was crushing me while he looked thrilled. He looked like my little boy again, the one who held my hand as we skipped to the swings and squealed with delight as he begged to be pushed higher.

18

Dr. Park was pleased with his progress. She was excited to work with him again once he was discharged and talked about signing him up for one of the latest research studies on nonviolent sexual offenders. I agreed, and more than once I almost told her what he was planning—what we were planning, since I had become part of his plan. It didn't feel right, but nothing had felt right in a long time. I'd lost my bearings. I wasn't sure if I'd ever get them back. In the end, I didn't tell her. It wasn't like she could stop him. Nobody could.

It wasn't easy to die painlessly. Most people thought you could take pills and sleep your way into death. It was the mistake Noah made the first time. In reality, most people who popped handfuls of pills ended up violently ill or having a seizure, but rarely dying. Most woke up with permanent brain damage. If he insisted on ending his life, I wanted it to be painless, easy, and successful. He deserved that. No more violent throwing up or hanging himself from the balcony like a savage. Most importantly, I didn't want him to do it alone. Nobody should have to die alone.

A dose of Nembutal would make him fall asleep and slowly decrease his respirations until he quit breathing. He'd fall asleep and never wake up. It was painless and the drug of choice in assisted suicides. But it was illegal, and no one could ask for Nembutal without raising eyebrows. Even though nurses called in prescriptions for doctors all the time, I'd walk out of the pharmacy in handcuffs if I tried to call in a Nembutal prescription under the name of one of the doctors I transcribed for. Even if I somehow managed to get my hands on a prescription, there was always an autopsy after the death of a child who died outside of a hospital setting, and they'd find it in his system. Everyone would wonder where he'd gotten it, and it wouldn't take long for them to connect the dots leading to me. I couldn't go to prison, so I had to make sure I didn't implicate myself in any way.

My only choice was to do something with the medications we already had. Normally, that would've consisted of Tylenol, Midol, cough syrup, and allergy pills, but I had a small pharmacy in my medicine cabinet given all the stress and turmoil of the last few years. I had a three-month prescription for Ambien and plenty of Xanax. I even had the anti-nausea medication he'd need to keep him from throwing up. I hadn't refilled my Xanax in over a year because I didn't like the way it made me feel, so I'd just learned to live with perpetual anxiety instead. But Ambien and Xanax weren't a strong enough combination to shut down his system without him waking up or getting sick. I was going to have to call my doctor and ask for something stronger than Ambien to help me sleep. It'd be relatively easy to talk him into prescribing something stronger, like Seconal, especially with everything that'd happened recently. They would find all the pills in his bloodstream, but no one would suspect I'd given them to him.

His last few days in the hospital dragged. We'd run out of things to say and spent most of our time sitting silence. I didn't know who I was anymore. What would happen to my insides after I helped end his life? Would I be too wrecked to function? There was nothing but uncertainty in front of me, and I had no idea how to feel.

Noah, on the other hand, looked more peaceful than he had in years. He was giddy and full of excitement the day he was released. He practically bounced as he walked out of the hospital.

"Okay, so what are we going to do?" His eyes were wild with anticipation on the drive home. "I can't believe the day is finally here. Ugh, you have no idea how long I've been waiting for this."

"What are you hungry for? Chinese? Thai?" I wasn't hungry, but we hadn't eaten since breakfast since all the discharge paperwork took longer than expected.

"I just want to get home. I don't care about eating."

"You've got to be starved. Aren't you sick of hospital food?"

He laughed. "Yeah, but who cares about food now? I can't wait to get home and do it."

I swerved into the other lane of traffic, nearly missing another car. "Noah, we're not doing *it* today." I gripped the wheel, forcing myself to stay focused on the road.

His face fell. "We're not?"

I shook my head.

"But I don't get it. I thought you agreed. What are we waiting for?"

I wrestled with my emotions, forcing myself to keep them at bay. "Well, there's a few pretty important things we need to take care of. We have to get your medication, and we have to do it in a way that keeps me out of it. I can't go to jail."

I pretended he was one of my patients rather than my son and launched into a clinical explanation of the combination of sleeping pills, anxiety medication, and anti-nausea medication that he'd need to be sure he fell asleep without getting sick beforehand or having a seizure. I explained what I'd get and how I'd get it, the way he'd have to take it, and the things we'd need to do leading up to it to make sure nothing we did raised any red flags.

"Wow, Mom. You thought of everything," he said after I finished.

I shuddered. It was nothing to be proud of.

"So, after I take everything, it'll be like an hour, and it's over?"

His eagerness was almost more than I can bear.

"It should be as long as everything goes according to plan." Our plan had to work. I refused to consider the alternative.

"Will I be aware of anything going on or am I going to be totally knocked out?"

"It's hard to say what it'll feel like. You might be able to hear things, but you'll be too messed up to move or open your eyes."

"So, I might be able to hear?"

I shrugged. "Maybe."

"I'm totally working on a playlist."

He started rattling off the different types of music and songs he was going to put on his iPod, but I quit paying attention. It was too painful listening to him select the songs he thought would be most appropriate to die to. How could he think about the music to accompany the moment? We were supposed to be planning the music for his high school graduation. The food we'd prepare. The guests we'd invite. Not this.

"How long until you can get the prescription?" He had the wild-eyed look of a drug addict who could barely wait to get their next fix. I stopped looking at him. It hurt too much.

"I'll call it in on Monday while you're at the hospital." I didn't know why I said Monday. It didn't really matter what day. He didn't push further. "Don't you think we should tell your dad?"

"Why would we tell Dad?" He looked at me like I suggested he stab himself in the eye.

"Don't you want to explain things to him?" Despite my feelings toward Lucas, it seemed like the right thing to do.

He shook his head. "Dad already knows. He always has."

"What about telling him good-bye?"

He thought about it for a moment. "You know what I want?" He didn't wait for me to answer. "I want one final family day at the Navy Pier. I want to walk along the water and ride the Ferris wheel like we used to do. We haven't done that in so long. I loved our day trips there, and Katie probably doesn't remember them since we haven't been there in so long. That's how I want to remember Dad."

I always loved our trips to the pier, especially during the summer. The views of Lake Michigan were some of the best in the state. Noah's favorite attraction was the maze with all its tunnels and obstacles, and Katie loved digging in the dinosaur sand pits inside the Children's Museum. I loved the Crystal Gardens. They'd always been special because Lucas took me there on one of our first dates.

"How about we go next weekend?" I asked.

"Sure. That sounds good. And then we can do it? Like that Monday?"

"You don't want any more time?" It was only nine days.

He grimaced. "That's like over a week away."

"I think you can make it until then."

"I guess if I have to."

I wasn't sure if I could. I didn't know if I could make it through any of this.

*****

I was worried being back at the apartment would be hard for him, but he was happy. He helped me make dinner, and we joked and laughed as we prepared my famous fried chicken. It was a secret recipe that'd been in my family for years. He ate ferociously as if he'd been starving for years. He gobbled up the chocolate cake we made for dessert.

"Didn't you say there's a flea market around here on Saturdays?" he asked as we did the dishes. I washed while he dried.

"Yes." I handed him another plate.

"Can we go tomorrow? We can grab breakfast beforehand like we used to do."

"Sure." I couldn't keep the surprise out of my voice. I wasn't sure what I expected us to do when he got home, but it wasn't flea market shopping. It was such an odd choice. Whenever we went before, I hunted for things for the house while he dug through clothes, searching for vintage t-shirts. What would he buy now?

The next morning he skipped through the market, searching for hidden treasures like we used to do, finding little knickknacks for the apartment, and bringing them to me as if he'd found a prize. I watched in bewilderment as he pawed through the piles of clothes. He walked with a confidence in his body that hadn't been there in so long. It was as if he'd been an empty balloon and someone filled him with air again. He made eye contact with people and smiled easily. He was like the Noah I remembered—the little boy I dressed up on Halloween, whose knees I kissed when they got skinned, and whose pillow I slid money under from the tooth fairy long after he believed in her existence—the one I'd given up ever getting back.

I was even more shocked when he wanted to go to mass on Sunday and insisted on bringing Katie with us. I was surprised when Lucas answered the door dressed in a collared shirt and tie. He sheepishly looked down and shrugged his shoulders.

"She insisted I go," he said.

We hadn't been to church as a family since before Noah's confession even though we used to go every Sunday. I kept stealing glances at Lucas while we drove, wondering what he was thinking. Did he have any idea what we were planning? In our entire marriage, I'd never kept a secret from him. Not even anything small. He looked as uncomfortable as I felt.

I scanned the sanctuary as we walked in and breathed a sigh of relief that I didn't recognize anyone. It was a small church, not like our old church in Buffalo Grove. Most of the rows were filled with senior citizens and not the rows of families we were used to. I dipped my hand in the holy water out of habit, making the sign of the cross without thinking. It was incredibly disorienting to be doing something we used to do so regularly back before everything fell apart. We slid into our seats, Lucas and I bookends on each side of the kids. Katie hadn't let go of Noah's hand since we stepped out of the car, and she cuddled up next to him on the pew.

As the liturgy of the readings began, the words that used to roll so easily off my tongue were gone. I couldn't bring myself to say, "Thanks be to God." The whole point of saying thank you was to acknowledge all God has done for us and his ability to speak through his Word. God hadn't done anything for my family or me in a long time. I listened to the chants around me, but the proclamations of faith didn't bring me any comfort. They were empty recitations with no meaning.

Unlike me, Noah's voice joined the congregation with force and confidence. He didn't miss a beat when we shifted into the hymns and moved his finger along the lines so Katie could follow along with him. She beamed. Both of them were tone-deaf, but they belted out the notes anyway.

I robotically followed the service, moving up and down on cue, but was remote and distant from the ceremonious rituals that used to fill me with peace and purpose. My eyes were drawn to the center stone of any Catholic church—the giant Jesus on the cross with a crown of thrones around his head and limbs nailed to the wood with spikes. Was everything I believed about God wrong too? My religion felt foolish, like I was a kid who found out Santa Claus wasn't real. I wanted to get up and never come back, but both my kids were happy, and their happiness had always been so much more important than my own, so I followed through each step, even receiving the Eucharist at the end. It left a bitter taste on my tongue.

Katie wanted us all to go out to lunch together, but Lucas couldn't get away from Noah and me fast enough. He looked like he wanted to jump out of his skin throughout the entire service.

"Please, Daddy," she begged, pulling on his arm as we walk to the car.

He wiggled his arm loose and tousled her hair. "I have lots of work to do today. We'll do it another time."

"But I've barely got to spend time with Noah, and I never get to see him." Her eyes filled with tears.

"I'm sorry, kiddo. Not today. Can you get in the car?" His face was pinched.

She folded her arms across her chest in a huff. "I hate this!"

Noah knelt next to her. "How about we all spend the day together next Saturday as a family? Mom and I were talking about going to the Navy Pier. It'd be really fun. We haven't gone in a long time."

Katie jumped up and down, squealing. "Please! Please! Please! Can we have a family day, Daddy, please?"

Lucas glared at me. I shrugged my shoulders. I hadn't talked to Noah about how we'd talk his dad into spending the day at the Navy Pier. Maybe this had been his plan for today all along.

"Fine, we can go," Lucas said.

"Promise?"

"Katie, come on. We need to get home." He opened the back door and motioned for her to get in.

She shook her head and crossed her arms across her chest. "You have to promise."

He rolled his eyes. "Okay. I promise. Now get in the car."

*****

I crept into Noah's room that night.

"Noah? Are you awake?" I whispered in case he was asleep.

"I'm awake."

I moved my way to his bed as my eyes adjusted to the darkness. I took a seat on the end of his bed, smoothing out the comforter. I'd never gotten around to buying him a new one. Now I never would.

"Are you scared?" The darkness fell like a blanket over our conversation, and it was easy to ask him in the dark when I couldn't see into his eyes.

"I was, but I'm not anymore."

"Where do you think you'll go?" I might have lost my faith in God, but I hadn't lost my fear.

"I don't think I'm going to hell if that's what you're asking me. I'm not saying I'm getting into heaven, but I know if there really is God, then he's got to know my heart. And he knows I'm doing the right thing, that I'm protecting lots of people from getting hurt."

Relief washed over me. I was glad he'd thought about this part. It made me feel better that he wasn't afraid of the afterlife even if I was terrified.

"I know we all have to pay for our sins. I totally get it, and it's right. We should have to pay, but I've paid for mine. If anyone's paid, it's me. But I shouldn't have to keep paying, and other people definitely don't need to keep being punished for what I've done and who I am."

I always thought suicide was the most selfish act a person

could commit, and that it was a complete disregard for others and the effect it would have on the people who loved them. I assumed people who did it were only thinking about themselves, but it wasn't the case with Noah. As I listened to him talk, I realized he wasn't just thinking about himself. He was thinking about everyone he cared about. Me. Katie. Even his dad, even though his dad no longer cared about him. It didn't matter. He still wanted good things for him. And he wasn't just thinking about us. He was thinking about people he didn't even know, nameless girls he might potentially harm.

"I want you to be proud of my choice."

I reached for him and brought him close to me.

"I am," I said. I'd never been more proud or loved him any more than I did at that moment.

19

"Did you get it?" He pounced on me as soon as I opened the door before I had a chance to set the bags of groceries down.

I shook my head.

"What happened?"

"I got scared. It didn't feel right."

I hadn't been able to call in the prescription. I spent all day while he was at the hospital staring at my phone. I picked it up over ten times but couldn't bring myself to tap my doctor's name.

"I'll do it tomorrow."

He shrugged. "Okay. I guess it doesn't really matter as long as we have it in time." He reached out to grab my bags of groceries and started helping me put things away. He hummed while he worked.

"How was therapy today?" I asked. "Was it weird to be back there?"

"Not really. It was nice knowing I didn't have to sleep there tonight, but group was pretty interesting. They got a bunch of new patients in over the weekend."

I stared at him like I'd been doing all weekend as he launched into a description of the new patients in the hospital. He was so happy. This morning he'd asked if we could go swimming at the YMCA and had called to find out the open swim times during one of his breaks at the hospital. How could he want to die when he was feeling so good? When things were so much better?

And then it dawned on me like I'd been stunned with a Taser gun. His excitement and zest for life weren't about being out of the hospital and feeling good again. He was happy because his fight was almost over. He was going to die soon and he couldn't wait. He acted like he did as a kid during the last two weeks leading up to Christmas when he counted every day and marked them off the calendar until the night Santa would arrive and deliver his presents under the tree.

It broke my heart that the only thing bringing him happiness was knowing he was going to die. He didn't just want to die—he was ready. My last bit of resistance dissolved. I called my doctor as soon as I dropped him off at the hospital the next morning. He listened patiently while I described Noah's hospitalizations.

"I haven't slept more than a few hours in a week. The Ambien has almost no effect on me anymore," I said just like I had practiced. "I'm sure it's because of everything going on with Noah again, and I've been taking it for so long that I've developed a tolerance."

"I totally understand." I could sense him nodding his validation through the phone. "What were you thinking?"

My heart banged in my chest. "I was thinking maybe I needed something stronger, just for a couple of nights so I can sleep. Maybe we could try a small dose of Seconal? If that doesn't work, then I'm pretty sure I'll never be able to sleep again." I forced a laugh, hoping it sounded real.

"Are you sure you want to have that in the house? I mean, with Noah being so suicidal?"

"Believe me, I've thought about that, and I'm not letting it out of my sight. Every pill in the house is locked up. Anything he could hurt himself with is hidden where he can't find it. I feel like I'm living in a psych ward myself, but I'm not taking any chances."

"That's smart. Really smart," he said. "Can I do anything else for you? Anything to make this easier for you?"

"Thank you, that means a lot. We'll get through this."

"Okay, so I'll call this in today. Let's check in at the end of the week to see how you're doing and make sure you're not having any side effects."

"Absolutely. Thank you."

My heart pounded so loudly while I waited to pick it up at the pharmacy that I was sure people could see it through my clothes. I was covered in sweat on the short drive home and certain at any moment the police were going to pound on the door and put me in handcuffs.

Noah ran out of his bedroom. "Is that it? Did you get it?"

I nodded, throwing the white bag on the table as if it would burn me if I held it much longer. He skipped over to the table, ripped open the bag, and pulled out the pill bottle. He twirled it around in his hands, marveling at them like he was holding a million dollars. A wide smile spread across his face, exposing his perfectly straight teeth from the years of braces. He set them back on the table and bounced over to me. He threw his arms around me, lifted me off the floor, and twirled me around.

"Thank you, Mom. Thank you so much."

"Put me down now." I couldn't keep my anger out of my voice.

He set me down, staring at me with confusion. "What's wrong?"

"You don't have to be so happy about it." I turned and ran to my room before he saw my tears.

I didn't come out of my room for dinner. He knocked at my door, but I told him I had a headache and needed to rest. There was nothing left to hold on to. I was losing my son for good. I was going to live the rest of my days never seeing his face, hearing him laugh, or the sound of his voice. I'd say his name, and he'd no longer respond. I was intensely aware of the hole he'd leave in my heart when he was gone, and it filled me with excruciating pain.

Sometime during the night, he crept into my bedroom like I crept into his a few nights before. He curled up next to me in my bed. His body longer than mine.

"I'm sorry, Mom. This has to be hard on you," he whispered.

I stifled a sob. "I'm going to miss you so much."

This time he was the one to hold me while I came apart in his arms.

20

The day was here. There was no going back. I didn't need to set an alarm clock because I hadn't slept, just paced the small apartment back and forth, treading a path across the worn carpet. It was like standing on the train tracks and bracing myself for the train about to hit. I kept checking on Noah, but he slept soundly with a peaceful smile tugging at the corners of his mouth. I spent hours during the night watching him sleep like I used to when he was a baby. He made the same grunting noises he made then.

I hadn't taken my eyes off him all weekend. During our family trip to the Navy Pier on Saturday, he took everything in like he was experiencing it for the first time. He gulped it all in hungrily like he was taking pictures to bring with him. The lake. The sun. Feeling the water on his skin like he did when he was a baby. He was completely enthralled. I'd never seen him look so alive.

We packed as much as possible into the day. Noah and Katie shared their comic books pages in the backseat as we drove, their endless chatter and laughter the soundtrack for our ride. We ate breakfast at the small diner right next to the pier before any of the tourists showed up. Noah scarfed down his pancakes and eggs. His appetite had been insatiable, and he'd added a few pounds back on his wiry frame. His cheeks no longer looked sunken in, and some of the color was back in his face. Lucas and I had coffee as we watched them eat, an unspoken understanding to get through the day with civility.

We hit all our favorite spots. We spent the morning at the Children's Museum, and even though Noah had long outgrown the activities, he walked Katie through each one like he was experiencing it for the first time. Lucas and I trailed after them like casual observers. We'd lost the ability to make small talk with each other, choosing instead to be silent. It was less awkward that way. By the time we finished the museum, it was time for lunch, and we let Katie pick the spot.

She chose pizza, which was no surprise since she'd eat cheese pizza for every meal if we let her. We took our slices with us and strolled down the long boardwalk, munching away as we walked. Lucas bought Katie a purple balloon—her favorite color—when she finished and helped Noah tie it on her wrist. We followed her as she skipped down to the beach.

We spent hours combing the beach for shells to add to our collections, competing for who could find the best one. Our house held jars of shells from different vacations we'd taken over the years. We made it a point to stop at beaches no matter where we vacationed. The kids waded into the water even though it was freezing and it'd be a long time before the water warmed, but it didn't matter to them. I sat on a rock and watched them frolic together, my recording brain taking it all in like I'd been doing all week.

We made our way back up to the boardwalk and watched as they jumped over the spouts of water shooting out from the sidewalk, strategically timing their jumps in an attempt not to get wet and failing miserably time and time again. Their love for each other encompassed them. You could almost reach out and touch it. Their smiles were better than any of the ones on the postcards you could buy in the shops lining the lakeshore.

I looked at Lucas. There was nothing that could move us more quickly to tears than watching the two people we loved more than anyone else in the world be completely in love with each other. We'd shared so many of these beautiful moments. The unspoken understanding of the innocent love we were witnessing always moved one of us to reach out for the other's hand—no need to speak, in case we broke the spell—to share the experience together.

I'd instinctively reached for his hand like I'd done so many times in the past. Our fingers used to slide together effortlessly like putting on a silk glove, but my fingers caught his the wrong way, and they twisted awkwardly with each other. He pulled his hand away without looking at me, stuffing both of them into his pocket. His face was stone.

"This is your last chance!" I wanted to scream so badly. The words threatened to spill from my mouth in a fiery tirade. *"This is it! There aren't any more days!"*

I wanted to save him from the agony that would come when he found out Noah was gone. When the news was delivered, and he was hit with the realization that he could have been in this moment. Everything that was in it and he'd missed it.

But I couldn't warn him. I could never let anyone know I played a role in Noah's death. Not even him. He couldn't have any part of it because of the remote chance they investigated Noah's death. Still, it didn't stop the impulse of wanting to shake him. Slap him. To wake him up to see what was right in front of him. What he was missing.

I didn't know if it was my imagination or not, but Katie held him longer than her normal, peel-her-off-him hug, as if somewhere in her unconscious she knew it was the last time she'd see him.

We spent yesterday like it was a normal lazy Sunday, which only increased the weirdness of the waiting. We did laundry, and it seemed absurd to fold his underwear and put it in his drawers, but I didn't know what else to do with them. We tidied up the house, but I refused to let him clean the bathroom even though he volunteered. Once his hairs disappeared from the sink, there would be none to replace them, and I couldn't bear the thought of washing him away.

"What are we going to have for my last supper?" he joked when dinnertime rolled around.

His ability to laugh about it was unsettling. In the end, we settled on pancakes smothered in my homemade syrup. The evening stretched out endlessly before us. Neither of us could stop looking at the clock. We pretended like we weren't but it was impossible not to. Each time it seemed a significant amount of time had passed, I'd look up only to discover it'd been a few short minutes since the last time I'd looked. It was odd that we were waiting. Would it really matter if we did it then? Did we really need to get a good night's sleep for suicide the next day? It seemed absurd to be stuck on the date we'd designated, but we were, and there was nothing left to do besides wait. We barely talked because there was nothing left to say. We'd said it all.

But now we stood in the doorway, surveying his bedroom. There was no going back once we crossed the threshold. We had spent one of our last nights talking about how he wanted it arranged, and everything was set up exactly how we'd planned. He even made his bed. His nightstand held the framed photo of our family standing at the edge of the Grand Canyon. It was one of our funnest summer vacations. We'd rented an RV and driven it across the country, stopping at all the tourist spots along the way. We'd parked on the Northern Rim, where the view was the most breathtaking, and spent three days hiking the trails. We'd all taken turns carrying Katie when she got too tired. I loved the picture.

Yesterday, I bought fresh flowers from Trader Joe's and put them in a vase on his dresser. We'd never gotten around to hanging anything on his walls, and I wanted him to have something pretty to look at. He laughed at me when I came home with the flowers, but his response was different today.

"Good call, Mom," he said. "They look nice."

"Thanks. Are you ready?"

He gripped my hand. Both of our hands were slippery with sweat. We didn't speak, the intimacy of the moment too intense for words. We stepped into the room.

I had never been so acutely present. My body hummed with energy. Tingling waves rushed through my body again and again, all of my senses on heightened alert. The wind coming from the open window tickled the hairs on my neck. The air carried the smell of breakfast from the neighbors down the street. Every bone in my body was alive. The sunlight streaming in through the small window above his bed looked exceptionally bright and vibrant. I could feel the warmth of it on my skin.

We moved to the bed, where all our materials were assembled and lay waiting for us on the serving tray I used back when I had visitors in my house to serve. I crushed all his pills yesterday, meticulously ground them into a fine powder. It was too many pills to swallow and it would be more effective to take them this way. They were piled on two round saucers. His antinausea medication lay next to them like you'd lay out clothes to wear the next day. My dropper, water bottle, and small glass stood ready. I motioned for him to sit on the bed next to the tray. He sat, straight-backed and at attention, placing his hands on his knees.

I crouched in front of him and took his face in my hands. I looked directly in his eyes. "Are you sure? Are you absolutely sure?"

He nodded his head while he spoke. "I'm more than sure—I'm so ready."

There was no going back. This was it.

I picked up the anti-nausea medication, the same kind they gave to chemotherapy patients to keep them from throwing up, and pulled back the lining on the tab. The dissolving tabs worked better than the pills. I laid the small tab on his tongue, eerily similar to how he received the Eucharist last Sunday.

"Can I swallow?" he asked as his mouth foamed.

I grabbed his chin and shut his mouth for him before any of it spilled out. "Yes, swallow it all."

He gulped it down. I laid another one on his tongue. I wasn't taking any chances with him getting sick and throwing up. I refused to consider what I would do then. This had to work. He knew what to do this time and swallowed it as soon as it started to foam.

Everything was in slow motion as I poured his pills into the small glass, dropping a few drops of water into it and stirring. Then, dropping a few more and stirring again until it was a consistency he could swallow without choking, but still as undiluted as possible.

We talked before about how he needed to take the pills, and I handed him the glass. I had another glass of water ready for when he finished. His eyes were wide with anticipation as I handed it to him. He plugged his nose and downed the concoction like he was taking a shot at a fraternity party that he'd never attend. He shuddered. I handed him the glass of water, and he quickly drained it. He wiped his mouth.

"What do we do now?" he asked. He set the glasses on his nightstand like we planned.

"We wait."

"I don't feel anything."

I smiled despite myself. "It takes more than thirty seconds. Just be patient. You will."

It didn't take long before a dreamy smile relaxed his face. My mind raced. Soon he would be too incoherent to understand anything, too drugged to speak. Was there anything I hadn't said? Adrenaline coursed through my body. What if I missed something? What if there was something important I'd never told him? The rush of responsibility to him, for this moment, coursed through me.

"*Dear God, please help us. Help my baby boy. Let this be*

easy. Please let him leave this world in peace." A sob caught in my throat. "*And please meet him there. Take care of him for me.*"

"You okay?" His voice was slurred like he had a mouthful of marbles to speak around.

I nodded, feeling the warmth of my tears running down my cheeks. Not the heat of the angry tears of struggle, but those of profound release. "I love you, Noah."

"I love you too, Mom." His lids were heavy, but there wasn't a hint of sadness or regret in his eyes. "Don't forget to give Katie her letter."

He'd given me two sealed letters earlier in the week. One for Lucas and one for Katie. I was supposed to give them to them afterward. I didn't know what they said and hadn't peeked because they were his private words to them.

"I won't. I promise. And Dad too."

"Can we turn on the music now?" His face lined with concentration as he struggled to form the words.

"Why don't you relax, honey?" I fluffed the pillows at the head of the bed and helped him lie down. He lay on his back with his arms crossed on his chest like a vampire. His arms looked too creepy arranged that way, so I placed them by his sides. He stared at the ceiling in a dreamy reverie. What was he seeing? He was here, but he was already somewhere else, with one foot in the now and the other in the later.

His iPod was plugged in on his nightstand next to the picture. I pressed play. As the first few notes of the Beatles sang out, his body relaxed into the bed. I crawled onto the bed beside him, sitting with my back against the headboard and pulled his head onto my lap. I held his hand. There was no more sweat. His hand was soft and warm in mine. He squeezed, and I smiled down at him. He smiled back, a weird lopsided grin.

"I love you, Noah," I said as I stroked his hair with my free hand.

His eyes rolled slowly up toward me, sluggish and hazy with all the drugs coursing through his system. He nodded, too high to speak. Keeping his eyes open took great effort, and eventually, he gave in to their descent.

I tuned into the music as I watched his chest move up and down. I had expected morose songs filled with despair and angst, but as I listened I realized it wasn't a playlist for him. It was for me. He recognized that while he was drifting away, I'd be acutely awake. The songs were for my benefit. Not his.

He started with the family favorite, "Here Comes the Sun," that we sang throughout our house every spring when the snow we'd been buried under for months finally started to melt. Other Beatles songs were sprinkled throughout, coupled with not just my favorite bands but Lucas's and Katie's too. There were songs we danced to in the living room or belted out on our road trips to the Grand Canyon and Niagara Falls. The ones we'd listen to on the way home from meets to help relax us after a stressful competition. Toward the end, the Dixie Chicks began singing "Lullaby." It was the song I sang to both my children during my pregnancy. Noah teased me mercilessly about it the older he got. But there it was, their sweet voices singing out, "How long do you wanna be loved? Is forever enough? Is forever enough?"

His thoughtfulness moved me with such exquisite pain, but I wouldn't cry. Not until it was over and he was gone. The one thing I could give him was a face of comfort and filled with love. I welcomed him into the world in a room filled with love and light and I could give him the same gift as I walked him home. It was so intimate. I felt the same way I did in the delivery room in the moments before I pushed him out into the world—the profound rush of God giving him to me. Now it was my turn to give him back.

I watched him die again and again. His mind was ready to die, but his body didn't agree. His breaths grew further and further apart. Each time I was sure he'd breathed his last, he gasped for another. It wasn't a fitful breath. More like he forgot and suddenly remembered he needed to breathe. Sometimes his eyes fluttered open after the breath. I pulled him into my lap, cradling him next to me, our bodies intertwined, his head resting against my chest as I held him as close as he could get. I knew the next step. What he was waiting for.

"It's okay, honey," I whispered into his ear. "You can go now. It's all right to leave." I rocked him back and forth. "I'm going to be okay. You don't have to keep hanging on. You can let go."

I kept whispering it over and over again long after the music stopped and the only sound was my voice humming "Lullaby." I rocked and whispered. Rocked and whispered. And then, he was gone. There was finally no more air.

HIM(NOW)

I'm not sorry Noah's dead. I know that makes me a terrible father, but I can't help it. I won't pretend I'm sad that he's gone. My insides burned with hate and disgust every time I looked at him, whenever Adrianne said his name. I couldn't even stand to be in the same room as him. It wasn't his fault. Not at all. But I couldn't be around him because he reminded me of everything I'd forced myself to forget.

I spent years burying the memories of what I'd done and convincing myself I was cured. It was hard in the beginning, but it got easier after I went to college because I didn't have to be around children anymore and could throw myself into my schoolwork. Numbers were easy. They made sense and gave me order. My roommate teased me about how serious I was all the time, but I didn't care. I had to be. It kept the monster inside of me quiet.

I tried to give back to humanity for what I'd taken, so I cleaned ditches every weekend and volunteered at nursing homes whenever I could. I spent my summers building houses for families in need with Habitat for Humanity. It's where I met Adrianne.

I never considered telling her what I'd done. Not once. No one could ever know. It was too shameful. Disgusting. In those days, it was easy to keep it a secret. It wasn't like the world we live in now. Barely anyone had computers in their homes, and even the ones that did didn't have the Internet. There weren't any sexual offender registries, and since my parents were equally invested in nobody finding out, we kept my crimes hidden.

My mom picked me up from the treatment center, gave me a huge hug, and said, "I'm glad that you're better." She never spoke about it again and carried on like nothing had changed.

My dad refused to speak to me when I got home and pretended like I wasn't there. Being ignored hurt, but I didn't blame him for how he treated me. After all, he was the one who found me with my cousins.

My uncle Shawn lived on the farm next to us and the two of them worked the land together. Shawn had two daughters—a ten-year-old and an eight-year-old. I was always stuck watching them since I was so much older. I was sixteen and hated trying to find ways to entertain them all day while our dads labored in the fields, but back then, you didn't argue with your parents. You did what they asked.

To this day, I still don't know how it happened the first time. It was like I was possessed. One minute we were playing hide–and–seek in the barn, and the next minute I was behind the hay bales rubbing myself on Jamie. I told her it was part of the game, and she didn't ask any more questions after that. I swore I would never do it again. But I did. Again and again and again. To both of them. I'd lie in bed at night and promise God that it was the last time, but I couldn't stop myself. I just couldn't. I was out of control.

My dad unexpectedly came into the barn one afternoon and caught me molesting Jamie. He flung me off her and whipped me with his belt until I passed out. Jamie wouldn't stop screaming. I still hear her screams in my dreams.

Shawn was just as furious as my dad. He wanted to send me to jail, but my mom begged him not to. She promised to get me help. Shawn and my aunt finally agreed not to tell the authorities as long as my parents got me help and kept me away from my nieces. That's how I ended up at Reuters for nine months. It's where they sent all the bad kids. I don't know what kind of treatment Noah got, but I hope they moved beyond the shock therapy that I received as part of my therapy.

Things were never the same after I came home. Our family was torn apart. Shawn sold his land and moved his family to the northeast, as far away from us as they could get. They never spoke to my family again. My dad was crushed since Shawn had always been his best friend. My dad started talking to me again after I left home for college, but he never forgave me.

I was doing so well until Noah screwed everything up. I'd managed to convince myself I was normal. I liked having a family. Being a husband and a father brought me great joy. I never imagined my son would become just like me.

I never forgot there was a monster buried inside me, but as long as I didn't feed it, it stayed dormant. Being with Noah was like looking in a mirror and having everything I hated about myself stare back at me. He became the part of me that was vile and repulsive. Visiting him at Marsh brought up all the memories of being at Reuters—the electric shock therapy, the boys assaulted in the locker room during showers, the never-ending terror I lived with every day. It was too much. I couldn't go back there.

I try to make myself feel sad that he's gone, and over everything that happened. I try to force it. Conjure up some kind of emotion in myself, but I can't. The truth? I'm just relieved. I feel like I can breathe again. It's finally over. I can go back to pretending like I'm normal.

EPILOGUE

I slid into a seat near the back. I tucked my purse behind my legs on the bleacher, pulled out a book and set it on my lap, hoping everyone thought I was waiting for one of my children to finish their lesson. I scanned the pool, searching for him. It didn't take long before I spotted his red head bobbing up and down at the far end of the pool. He didn't look like Noah, but he had the same energy as he moved through the water. That's why I liked to watch him. I came every Tuesday at four.

It had been almost a year since Noah died and it was a lie that time healed all wounds. Whoever said it originally never lost a child. The wound cuts too deep to ever go away. I felt the magnitude of his loss as if it was yesterday—the paralyzing grief of losing a child. It came in waves, spastic sobs reverberating throughout my entire body, shaking me to my core. It was unrelenting and constant in the beginning. It held me in its grips and refused to let go. I felt like I would die, but I didn't because you can't die from grief even if it feels like you might. I stayed alive because my lungs kept breathing and my heart kept beating through no effort of mine. I didn't have any other choice.

Nobody told me grief became so unpredictable over time. I never knew when it was going to hit, so there wasn't any way to prepare for the attacks. The attacks had grown farther apart, but they'd never be gone, and I'd never be prepared. It didn't help to remind myself I'd survived them before and would survive them again because, in the moment, I was sure it was the one that would kill me.

But I had to go on for Katie, because being a mother means you live your life as a living sacrifice. Katie struggled as much as I knew she would. She cried for days when she found out, and we spent hours huddled together on the couch, taking turns crying or weeping unable to move from our spot. She refused to be alone even in the bathroom, and she'd always been an intensely private person. She followed Lucas and me from room to room like she'd done when she was a toddler. She slept with me at night, but I didn't mind having her so close because I needed her as much as she needed me. We clung to each other through the long sleepless nights and fitful dreams when our bodies had no choice, but to surrender to the exhaustion. I assured her we would get through it. I needed to say the words for her even if I didn't believe it.

I gave her Noah's letter and never asked to read it. It was his words to her, and I respected their relationship. She didn't tell me what he said, but it seemed to bring her comfort. She carried the letter with her everywhere, tucking it underneath her pillow at night. Within weeks of the funeral service, I got her into therapy with a child psychologist that Dr. Park recommended. It took a while, but she was beginning to get better. She stopped wetting the bed, which was a good sign. She kept a journal and wrote him letters every day.

Going back to school was the most difficult for her. She couldn't make it through the day without sobbing uncontrollably over something insignificant like misspelling a word or breaking her pencil lead. Other times, she sat in her chair or on a space on the red carpet, immobilized. She never made it to lunchtime without her teacher calling me to come pick her up and bring her home. I didn't know how to help or save her, until I stumbled on the blog of a woman who'd lost her daughter to cancer. She'd created necklaces with all her surviving children to serve as living memories of their sister and something they could touch whenever they missed her. I loved the idea.

Katie and I spent an entire weekend picking out our charms and beads, threading each one carefully on the wire until we were finished and each had a necklace. We called them our "remember Noah" charms. We never took them off and rubbed them whenever we felt sad. Touching the beads was inherently calming, and it was the turning point for her. She was finally able to make it through a full day at school.

She seemed more and more like herself every day, but her eyes bore the weight of his ghost. I didn't know if there would come a day when she had more questions for me, but it wasn't here yet. I didn't know what I'd explain to her when she was an adult, but I couldn't think that far into the future. The challenge of getting through each day was enough.

Lucas was relieved Noah was gone. He'd never said it, but it was written all over his face. Every time his eyes came across the pictures I refused to take down from around the house, I saw the relief wash over him. I gave him his letter and was too afraid to ask if he'd read it in case he said no. It was better not to know. He wouldn't come with me to pick out the urn for Noah's ashes and moved it back on the dresser in my room no matter how many times I put it on top of the fireplace. Eventually, I quit trying. Now, his urn sat on top of my dresser next to the picture I framed from our last day at the Navy Pier, where Noah beamed with happiness surrounded by his family.

I'd moved back into their house, but our marriage was over. We both knew it, even though we didn't talk about it because living together under the guise of being together was the best thing for Katie. She needed both of us. Her parents splitting up on top of what she'd been through would be selfish and cruel, so we forced ourselves to live together despite how we felt about each other. I couldn't bring myself to sleep next to him, though. The thought of being that close to him made my skin crawl. He stayed in the master bedroom, and I moved into the guest bedroom.

We no longer had real conversations. Our hearts were too hardened toward each other. We moved around each other like cordial roommates. Our interactions were limited to talking about bills, errands, school pickups and drop-offs, appointments, and other practical stuff. There would come a time when we divorced and walked away from each other, but that time wasn't now.

I'd joined the ranks of mothers who'd watched their children die—a mom's club I never thought I'd be a member of during my days on the PTA. I sought solace in grief support groups because the only people who understood what it was like to lose a child were other parents who had. As I listened to their heart-wrenching stories, I was grateful not to be left with any unanswered questions or burdened with the pain of regret. All my questions were answered. No stone unturned. I wasn't plagued with trying to figure out why or what he was thinking in his last moments. I didn't have to spend my time pining over the things I wished I'd said to him. Without knowing it, Noah gave me a great gift, but it didn't relieve the guilt.

The guilt would never go away. Not over what we did. I didn't regret what I did for him. Never would. The remorse came when I started taking steps to begin living again. The first time I laughed after he was gone, I clamped a hand over my mouth as if I was betraying him. It didn't matter I knew he wanted me to enjoy my life and be happy. I still felt like I was betraying his memory.

A few months after he died, I was busy cleaning up the mess Katie and I made from baking cookies all afternoon, and suddenly, it hit me—I hadn't thought about him since I'd started cleaning up. Minutes had passed without any trace of him. I fell to my knees sobbing, begging him to forgive me for abandoning him. The longer the intervals grew, the guiltier I felt. There was no way to win. If he didn't consume my every waking moment, I felt like I was failing to keep him alive.

My biggest fear was that I'd forget parts of him, and he'd be taken from me piece by piece until I was left with nothing except an empty ache where he used to be. It terrified me to lose anything about him and not remember every detail. His smile. His eyes. The smell of his hair. The way he looked at Katie. How he sounded when he called me Mom. Being his parent didn't stop after he died, and it was my job as his mother to protect his memory in the same way I protected him while he was alive.

After he died, it was like I'd been speeding in a car going ninety miles per hour and somebody opened the door and threw me out. I stood in the road profoundly disoriented as the world spun around me while I stayed still. I couldn't count the number of times Noah said that I'd get my life back after he was gone, but I was forever changed. The previous version of myself was utterly destroyed. I didn't know what returning to my life meant. The empty chair at the dining room table was a continual reminder of all I'd lost.

In the days leading up to his death, I thought I'd spend all my time after he was gone thinking about him when he was a little boy. But that wasn't the case. I replayed memories of him when he was young, but much of my time was spent replaying our last moments together and how he let me step into his soul, to know him more than I knew anyone else and to love him. Death was intensely private, and I'd never felt so close to another human being as I did when I held him during his final minutes.

I'd found my way back to God, a place I never thought I'd be again. It wasn't out of a deep faith or a profound spiritual experience, but out of pure necessity to believe God existed. If he didn't exist and this was the end, then I never got to see Noah again, and I refused to believe that. There had to be a God, because there had to be a heaven. A time when I got to see him again, and he was the one to walk me home.

ABOUT THE AUTHOR

Dr. Lucinda Berry is a clinical psychologist and leading researcher in childhood trauma. She uses her experience to weave psychological thrillers that blur the lines between fiction and nonfiction. She is the author of PHANTOM LIMB, APPETITE FOR INNOCENCE, and MISSING PARTS. She lives in Los Angeles with her husband and son. You can find her on Facebook or https://about.me/Lucindaberry.

Made in the USA
Middletown, DE
27 November 2022